W9-DGH-359

AGAINST THE CURRENT

AGAINST

As I Remember

DONALD S. ELLIS • PUBLISHER

THE CURRENT

F. Scott Fitzgerald

by Frances Kroll Ring
Foreword by A. Scott Berg

CREATIVE ARTS BOOK COMPANY · 1987

Copyright © 1985 by Frances Kroll Ring
Scottie Fitzgerald Smith's prefatory comment copyright © 1985 by Scottie
Fitzgerald Smith.
Foreword copyright © 1985 by A. Scott Berg
Permission to quote from unpublished interviews by R.L. Samsell granted by
R.L. Samsell.

All rights reserved. Printed in the U.S.A.

No part of this publication may be reproduced or transmitted in any form or by
any means, electronic or mechanical, including photocopy, recording, or any
information storage and retrieval system now known or to be invented, without
permission in writing from the publisher, except by a reviewer who wishes to
quote brief passages in connection with a review written for inclusion in a
magazine, newspaper or broadcast.

Published by Donald S. Ellis, San Francisco,
and distributed by Creative Arts Book Company.
For information contact:
Creative Arts Book Company
833 Bancroft Way
Berkeley, California 94710

ISBN 0-88739-015-3
Library of Congress Catalog Card No. 85-047682

First paperback edition 1987.

To Jennifer and Guy
From Mom

As THE DAUGHTER of two allegorical figures of pre-World War II America, I confess I have developed an allergy to reading about my star-crossed parents. But this memoir by Frances Kroll Ring, my father's secretary, crutch, and confidante during his last years, is so charming, and so obviously heartfelt, that I couldn't help enjoying it.

The author presents a vivid personal recollection of a man wrestling with his private devils, finally losing the battle—though winning the war. I think my father would be more pleased by knowing that he kept her affection and respect throughout than by any other reassurance which may have reached him in that special corner of Heaven reserved for tormented artists.

Scottie Fitzgerald Smith
1985

FOREWORD

EVEN F. SCOTT FITZGERALD'S most devoted fans must
wonder if there is anything left to write about his life.
Since Arthur Mizener exhumed him in 1951 with *The
Far Side of Paradise*, scores of biographies and critical
studies have been written on the subject, raising him
from obscurity to this side of sainthood. In the last
twenty-five years alone there have been no less than
three major biographies of Fitzgerald: Andrew Turnbull
constructed a sturdy life story, only slightly varnished by
his own adolescent reminiscences of the man; André Le
Vot, a Frenchman, spent two decades at his canvas, a
detailed mural of the American landscape in which
Fitzgerald flowered and faded; and Matthew J. Bruccoli,
in his five hundred page tome, *Some Sort of Epic
Grandeur*, delivered "more facts," stuff which had not
been contained in his dozen other volumes about
Fitzgerald.

The lives and loves of Scott Fitzgerald and his
equally mythic wife have been explored in Nancy
Milford's dramatic *Zelda*, James Mellow's eloquent
Invented Lives, the exuberant *Exiles from Paradise* by
Sara Mayfield, and Scott Donaldson's provocative *Fool
for Love*.

Most of Fitzgerald's letters to his family, friends,
editor, and agent have been published in one volume or
another, as have his notebooks, scrapbooks, and
financial books.

The century's greatest literary essayists, from Van
Wyck Brooks to Gore Vidal, have evaluated and

explicated Fitzgerald's writings. Edmund Wilson, Malcolm Cowley, Maxwell Geismar, and Afred Kazin have all analyzed his five novels and some one hundred fifty short stories in the context of his life. Aaron Latham has written a lively account of Fitzgerald's retreats to Hollywood, *Crazy Sundays*; and Tom Dardis devoted several chapters to the same topic in *Some Time in the Sun*. There are dozens of other works on his works, including incisive studies by Henry Dan Piper, Robert Sklar, and Charles E. Shain. Another generation of Fitzgerald scholars and teachers—notably Alan Margolies and Jackson Bryer—keep discussion of his work alive; and some of their students, no doubt, will carry on the tradition.

Fitzgerald also appears in many people's memoirs. He is most prominent in Ernest Hemingway's unforgettable (and to the most devout Fitzgerald readers, unforgivable) *A Moveable Feast*, Morley Callaghan's *That Summer in Paris*, Edmund Wilson's journals, and Malcolm Cowley's books of reminiscences. Sheilah Graham has kissed and told about Fitzgerald again and again and again and again.

And now Frances Kroll Ring, Fitzgerald's secretary during his final twenty months, has set down her memories of that time, thinking she has some new pieces to add to the jigsaw puzzle. She does—and even more . . .

Twenty-year-old Frances Kroll went to work for F. Scott Fizgerald at the apogee of his career, when he was as far from the public eye as he had ever been. During the next year and a half, she saw Fitzgerald almost daily. She did not encounter some Jazz Age cartoon character, a careless show-off wasting his talent; nor did she find the shell of a cracked-up author. Instead, she worked alongside a thoughtful and introspective writer in the throes of what promised to be his greatest novel. This most private side of the once public personality went completely unseen, except for the wide eyes of his secretary.

Almost everything Fitzgerald did in those twenty months made some impression on Frances Kroll; and fortunately for us she has been able to conjure up memory after memory of those days. In getting them on paper, she had no axes to grind, no horn of her own to blow. She has, instead, focused on Fitzgerald and presented a most vivid picture of the literary lion in autumn working like hell to put his life back together.

Fitzgerald had sojourned to Hollywood in 1927 and 1931; and he revisited Babylon in 1937, at the pinnacle of its glamour. He stayed, on and off, for the next two and one-half years. The town was irresistible, dazzling with untold riches and the most beautiful people on earth; and he was, for a while, under contract to a studio that boasted "more stars than there are in the heavens." But Fitzgerald lived a touchingly quiet life in one corner of the city or another. Frances Ring's recalling the quotidian details of that life in the San Fernando Valley and then in an apartment house set far back from Laurel Avenue will probably bring readers closer to him than any book has thus far. On each page (Just wait until you read Fitzgerald's method for killing a carp so that Frances's mother can make gefilte fish!) you can practically feel him standing there, reading over your shoulder.

F. Scott Fitzgerald was virtually bereft of his family during his last years, owing to his wife's breaking down and his daughter's growing up. From the other books that have been written, one feels melancholy that the Fitzgeralds could not go home again; with Zelda in and out of mental institutions and nineteen-year-old Frances Scott (known to the world as Scottie) at Vassar, they seemed fated never to be all together again.

For me, the most haunting and heartening image in *Against the Current* is that of Sheilah Graham and Frances Kroll drawing closer each day to Scott Fitzgerald, becoming the spouse and daughter that had slipped away. After everything Fitzgerald had endured in his short life, it is comforting to see him at the end surrounded by a surrogate family, in the company of a loving new belle—vivacious and blond, just as Zelda had been—and a petite twenty-year-old—smart and full of curiosity . . . and even named Frances.

So here's one more look at F. Scott Fitzgerald, perhaps the clearest glimpse you will ever get—because it's pure Fitzgerald, one hundred proof.

A. Scott Berg

Los Angeles
Spring, 1985

AGAINST THE CURRENT

*So we beat on, boats against the current, borne
back ceaselessly into the past.*
                                        The Great Gatsby

F. Scott Fitzgerald in Encino, 1939

Frances Kroll in 1939

Scottie Fitzgerald, Fred Astaire and Helen Hayes in Hollywood, 1937

Winning Editor, College Bazaar
August 1940

Photographs courtesy of Scottie Fitzgerald Smith

PRELUDE

THERE IS A BIRD outside my window. It nibbles at a leaf, looks about, picks up a twig, drops it, flits to a tree, finds another twig, then flies off to build its nest. I feel akin to the bird as I sift through my scattered keepsakes trying to assemble a memoir of the last twenty months of the life of F. Scott Fitzgerald.

So much has been written about him that I hesitate to add another word. Yet, during those last months, I was his personal secretary and saw him daily. Though I have recorded the experience in a few short articles and have answered the queries of many biographers, I feel a need to do some pencilling in, some touching up, some strengthening of the existing portrait so that it more clearly comes into focus as the man I knew.

I will necessarily repeat certain familiar data and will probably not be objective. My opinions are intensified over a forty-year period and are biased in Fitzgerald's favor. I was young and unworldly when I worked for him, but I did have the sense to recognize that Scott Fitzgerald was no ordinary man. A certain luster clung to his diminishing reputation even then. Just being caught in that fading light made up for the endless chores and erratic demands of the job.

"Why do you run every time he calls you?" my parents would ask. "What kind of work is this? What kind of hours?"

It was difficult to explain. When he needed you, he

needed you now. He lived under gathering clouds and the storm was always threatening. Though his talent lay within him like a deep well, there were dry spells that had nothing to do with his writing ability but were the effects of kaleidoscopic life patterns, sometimes so jumbled that the energy he spent controlling the fragments diverted him from the creative course.

He wished for immortality and the verbal music he made early on held out the possibility of that wish fulfillment. But when he died at age forty-four, there was no indication that his imprint would outlive him. Now there are twenty-nine books about Fitzgerald on my shelf and they are but a fraction of those listed in his bibliography.

What makes him the object of such ongoing attention? Certainly, he personified a moment in time and his reputation has become an idiom that immediately evokes an era—both literary and trivial. A Gatsby-like silk robe has a price tag of $450. A bar named F. Scott's speaks easily for itself.

For me, he also left a touch of magic, intriguing us continuously to try to fathom his cleverness. His heroes and heroines were always more than they seemed to be; his vision of them was clear but he played with colors that often diffused their images; his sleight of hand enchanted rather than deceived. Again and again, he pulled a name, a voice, a phrase out of the air and let it rest on a page. The technique was smooth; the effect belied the effort it took to make it come out right.

There were the deeds, too—the generous spirit, the genuine interest in people who walked through his life, even briefly. Fitzgerald was not a humanist in a large, sociological sense. He was not an active participant in social causes though he understood their relevance. But he cared deeply for those who came within his orbit and was attentive to their needs. That concern is reflected in his letters, in his friendships.

My memory harbors a gentle man with a nearly collapsed dream whose prevailing gift gave him the strength to keep doing what he did best—to write.

AGAINST THE CURRENT

By rule of hour and flower,
By strength of stern restraint
  And Power
To fail and not to faint.
            —Alfred Noyes

APRIL, 1939. It was spring in the San Fernando Valley. The air was fresh and cool; the surrounding hills were flushed with new green. Ventura Boulevard was a two-lane road that cut through miles of undeveloped ranchland. I drove along in a state of exhilaration, on my way to an interview for a secretarial job.

After weeks of making the rounds, I had just this morning wandered into Rusty's Employment Agency on Hollywood Boulevard and filled out an application. There were no other job seekers in the small office. Rusty, auburn-haired and smartly dressed, interviewed me. She noted my limited experience, but I emphasized my typing and dictation speeds and my interest in working for a writer.

Rusty sized me up—young, confident with a touch of shyness. If my skills were as good as I indicated on the application, she might have something for me.

She asked if I knew who F. Scott Fitzgerald was.

I did.

What did I know about him?

Not much, I admitted. I had read a few of his stories in magazines. I thought he lived in Paris.

He was now living in Los Angeles, she told me, and was looking for a secretary who was not a Hollywood person.

I did not understand.

He did not want anyone who had worked for the film studios.

Aah. Well, I had recently moved to Los Angeles from New York with my parents and had only done some freelance manuscript typing for screenwriters.

Would I mind working at the author's home rather than in an office?

No. That seemed to be the pattern out here.

Rusty phoned to make sure Fitzgerald was available, gave me directions, and sent me on my way.

I had no idea what he would be like. If only I had read his books. A tinge of nervousness came over me as I sighted the storefront post office and small market that identified Encino. I turned right on Amestoy Avenue to a tree-lined country lane that led to 5521, the Edward Everett Horton Estate which he called "Belly Acres." Horton was an actor—a prissy-voiced comedian—who had wisely invested his money in land. The big manor house sat on a knoll looking over a white guest cottage that he had rented to Fitzgerald. I parked in the driveway and went through the garden gate. Pink roses climbed the fence surrounding the house. I rang the bell. A black woman admitted me. While I waited, I caught a glimpse of an enormous living room that went from one end of the house to the other. It was filled with period furniture and resembled a salon.

The woman returned and showed me up the stairs. There, sitting in an antique bed, was F. Scott Fitzgerald. I was not prepared for the poetic, handsome face. I had expected him to be older. The faded, blond hair and pale skin were signs of middle age or illness. The eyes were very blue and inquiring. He nodded in greeting—a funny little gesture, as if he were doffing a hat except that he wasn't wearing one. He asked me to come in and sit by the window.

I hesitated. I had never been interviewed in a bedroom before.

Would I forgive him for not getting up? He had a fever. He was quick to assure me that he was not contagious. I had yet to learn about his fevers. He asked about my experience and wanted the names of the writers I had worked for. When I mentioned Herman Mankiewicz, he perked up. "I love Mank," he said, "but I don't want anyone who has MGM contacts." I emphasized that I had never been hired by the studio, but had worked for him at home on special projects. He could phone for a reference.

Fitzgerald said that wouldn't be necessary and explained why he was making such a point about the studios. In a confidential voice, he told me that he was planning to start a new novel about the motion picture industry and wanted no word of it to leak out. He needed a secretary who wouldn't gossip to movie people, who would be absolutely trustworthy. He then asked me to open the bottom drawer of a bureau next to my chair. I did. Instead of shirts or underwear or whatever one might expect to find in a bureau drawer, there were gin bottles. I was confused and made no connection between the bottles and Fitzgerald. I didn't know he was an alcoholic. My image of alcoholics was of vagrants who lay around drunk in alleys or in New York's Bowery. I shrugged and closed the drawer.

Did I know why the bottles were there?

I didn't.

Fitzgerald did not comment.

I sat down again. He looked at me quizzically, probably trying to figure out where I had been all my life. Embarrassed by his stare, I smiled.

He then told me that he had a daughter at Vassar. Had I gone to college?

I hadn't and became defensive. I chose to support myself, I told him, so I went to a business school after graduating from high school. But I read a lot and took music lessons and joined an art workshop, I added quickly wanting very much to impress him. He listened attentively.

After a pause, he said that his daughter had a financial emergency—a frequent condition with her. As he was not well enough to go into town and wire her some cash, would I mind doing it for him? He would give me the money which I could take to a Western Union office and then telephone him when that was done. I said I would be glad to. He asked me to hand him his wallet which was on the bureau and counted out thirty-five dollars.

Did that mean I was hired? I asked timidly.

He said he would let me know and thanked me for helping him out.

On the drive back, I thought about the interview and didn't know what to make of it. He had asked me neither to take a letter nor to type anything. There were all those stories about Hollywood secretaries who couldn't type or spell. If it was going to be that kind of job, I'd quit. Quit? He hadn't even made an offer. Yet I hoped he would. He was certainly good-looking, and I was already charmed by his manner as well as intrigued by the possibility of being present at the start of a novel. No routine office job and better than taking a writing course at some junior college. I would be learning from a living author. I had better stop at the library and check out his novels so that I would be prepared. I instinctively knew I wouldn't tell him that I was more familiar with Hemingway. I had read *The Sun Also Rises*, which we discussed in my senior year at high school because of the controversial language and realistic style.

I was soon halfway through the valley and decided to take Laurel Canyon to Sunset Boulevard. The road snaked steadily upward through the mountain to a plateau called Mullholland Drive, then wound down the hill with here and there a small house of exotic design nested in the dense foliage. Working in the valley would be like driving to the country every day—no busses, no subway, no possible way to get there without a car. I had borrowed the family Pontiac for the interview. I'd have to make some arrangement with my father to use it for work until I had enough money to buy a car of my own.

I found a Western Union, filled out the necessary form and wired the money to Scottie Fitzgerald, Vassar College, Poughkeepsie, New York. Then I phoned Fitzgerald to report.

Once again, he thanked me, then asked, "Can you

come to work tomorrow at ten?"

Even though I'd been thinking about nothing else all the way back from the interview, I hadn't expected him to decide so quickly and I was slow to respond.

"Will thirty-five dollars a week be all right?" he asked.

Thirty-five seemed to be the magic number. It was also good pay in 1939. I accepted.

I didn't understand until later why he went through the elaborate scheme of sending me to town with the money and asking me to phone him back, if he had intended to hire me all along. It turned out that it was his way of testing my honesty. If I had gone off with the thirty-five dollars, it would have been a small loss. But I didn't; I carried out his request and proved I could be trusted. How could he have known that it would never have occurred to me to take the money?

■   ■   ■

From the start, this was not just another job. Even so, I could not foresee the influence it would have on my life, and I kept no diary. But I saved letters and notes and now, almost a lifetime later, I recall incidents with the warmth of remembrance rather than in chronological sequence.

People still ask "what was he *really* like?" as if they are unable to find satisfying answers in the Fitzgerald literature; as if his durability must be due to something more than his recording of the Roaring Twenties, more than his rapid decline in the thirties. So much emphasis has been placed on the antics of his alcoholism that shadows fall to darken a high-contrast image.

I wasn't around during the early success of the romantic youth who had a quick fame, more money than he dreamed he could earn, good looks and charm. By the time I knew him, it was hard times; the youth was middle-aged. Yet the glamor that had attached itself to Fitzgerald, and was synonymous with riches and society, still clung. He and Zelda *were* the Jazz Age and the evidence is there to prove that there were probably no two people around at the time who drank more, partied more, pranked more and abandoned themselves more to hedonism than Scott and Zelda. They laid the groundwork for the personal hell that followed—Zelda's breakdown and Scott's crackup. The times did the rest. The stock market crashed, the economic depression brought the whole country to a day of reckoning. Unemployment and breadlines were no subjects for romantic tales.

But romance was Scott's strength. *Tender Is The Night* was not an idea he could abandon. He struggled to conclude it while Zelda struggled with her schizophrenia at Highland Hospital in Asheville, North Carolina, where she lived, with only occasional holidays, for the rest of her life.

For their daughter, Scottie, it was summer camp from age eleven. "I'm not going to write you much this summer but you know my heart is with you always," Scott said. The rest of the year, she lived with him. It was not until she was fifteen that he made inquiries about boarding schools. He decided finally on Miss Ethel Walker's.

Scott was the sole breadwinner for this three-way family, a role he maintained with determination. There were no second thoughts. Zelda must have the best medical help available; Scottie must have the best schooling. He would pay for it, somehow. Hollywood was the somehow. Scott went west into the MGM lion's cage.

■   ■   ■

When I came on the job, he was finished with Hollywood—or it with him, except for an occasional assignment. His contract with Metro had lapsed. His contribution had been minimal.

Edwin Knopf, the MGM story editor who had brought him to the studio, said that no one worked harder or was more determined to succeed. He described Scott as "frighteningly gentle, with consummate grace and manners. He was like a fire in a grate—you went to him; he never sought you."

Though Scott was among several reputable novelists brought to the coast for their special talents, he did not cry corruption or abuse at film industry money. Hollywood was not responsible for the decline of his reputation, nor did it affect his writing even though Hollywood did not use him well. He needed the money. He felt he earned it and gave the scenarios his best shot. He was, in fact, fascinated by films, by the inner structure of the studios; its workings were continuing research for the novel that stirred within him. What he found offensive was having his writing tampered with by directors or rewritten by "hacks." Nor did he believe that he wasn't or couldn't be a good screenwriter despite the contrary opinion of his Hollywood agent, H.N. Swanson, who felt that Scott was "never at home in screenwriting. It was not his medium." Aside from that, Swanson loved Scott. "If you sat in a room with him, he'd give you the feeling that somewhere around the corner something exciting was gonna happen. He was warm and wonderful and producers were in awe of him."

Yet if he did not believe in Scott's screenwriting ability, how could he have "sold" him to a studio? No wonder Scott used to cuss out "Swanie" privately for not getting him work.

In that era of moviemaking, writers had little influence in Hollywood. The slogan was *action*, not words, and Scott was, essentially, a wordsman. He somehow got lost in the shuffle of studio treachery. However, he didn't pick up and go back home. He had no home to go back to. So he stayed on—a gentlemanly misfit in an unreal environment.

■　　■　　■

As a transplanted easterner, I also found Los Angeles unreal. I had come west, not by choice but out of filial obedience. My parents had celebrated their twenty-fifth winter wedding anniversary with a trip to Arizona followed by a short detour to Los Angeles. My father promptly fell in love with the June-in-January sunshine, the space, the cleanliness. By the time he returned home, his mind was made up. We were moving to California.

At first it seemed like madness. What would he do there? He was a furrier. Nobody wore furs in Los Angeles. There were movie stars, he said, who wore furs and there were studio designers who used furs in films.

It would be fine—not to worry. As long as he had his two hands, he could always make a living. The plan was for him to wind down his business in New York, then go to L.A., find a place to live, and rent a store. I would follow to help him set up shop, take care of his accounts and write letters for him. When we were settled, my mother and younger brother would follow.

So, in November of 1938, I answered his summons. A few weeks of palm trees, sun and beach and I began to miss New York, its vitality, activity and mobility. I missed my friends and I missed seeing people on the streets. Except for Hollywood and certain downtown areas, Los Angeles was sparsely developed.

Despite the klieg lights that sprayed the skies on film premiere nights attracting hundreds of fans who waited about to catch a glimpse of a movie star, there was little life after dark. I took a New Yorker's snobbish and dim view of Pasadena, which had a playhouse. Downtown Los Angeles had *one* major legitimate theatre—the Biltmore—where touring New York hits were housed for short runs. Big bands visited the Biltmore Hotel's Bowl and the Ambassador's Coconut Grove. Sunset Strip was two blocks of quaint one and two-story white shops and a Trocadero night club.

Hollywood celebrities were a breed apart. Their legendary parties took place in their palatial homes, behind gates. The stars certainly did not hang out at Hollywood and Vine. Neither did they come to the huge store that my father had rented on Wilshire Boulevard near St. Andrew's s Place and directly opposite Perino's, then the most elegant restaurant in Los Angeles. He was sure that the Perino diners would come and browse after lunch and look at his furs. Instead, they got into their cars and drove away. This was not Fifth Avenue. There were no pedestrians on Wilshire Boulevard. We spent hours looking out the window watching all the cars go by. Some days, out of boredom, I would try on the furs and parade in front of the mirrors. But each day without customers made the grey-blue carpeted "salon" seem larger and emptier. After three months, we closed down. Undaunted, my father went looking for opportunities to ply his trade. I did the same.

By this time, my mother and brother had joined us. The neighborhood where we lived—North Sycamore just east of La Brea Avenue, a main cross street—was totally residential, a mixed architectural hodgepodge of bungalows, cottages and duplexes of English, Spanish and Moorish design. Nothing stood over two stories high. All buildings appeared to be unoccupied although cars in the driveways indicated otherwise. There were no front porches and the only visible people were the Japanese gardeners who came in their trucks to tend the neat little lawns twice a week. There was no feeling of a community when you ventured down the street, and the prime attribute of this location was convenience. It was near a trolley line that started at La Brea Avenue and Third Street—just a two-block walk from our apartment. You could hop a car which ran along Third to downtown or transfer to a Hollywood line. There was a fairly regular daytime schedule, but at night you could be stranded for hours.

My major accomplishment was getting a driver's license, but the city's unwieldy geography made me hanker for the subways. I pointed one foot back toward

New York and kept it there until I started working for Fitzgerald. The job significantly changed my attitude and gave purpose to that time of my life.

■   ■   ■

I reported to Encino that April, 1939, eager to learn, ready to work. Fitzgerald, on the other hand, was not up to much activity. He was totally lacking in energy and spent the better part of each day in bed. Certainly my work in those first weeks had nothing to do with preparation for the novel which was to become *The Last Tycoon*. There was no routine, no regularity. Each day was different depending on how Scott felt, on his mood, on whether he had been able to sleep the night before or sleep it off.

The first thing I learned was that the water tumbler on his night stand was to be left alone. I had made an attempt to freshen it and he took the glass from me. The sweetish odor was not stale water, as I thought, but gin. Juniper berry permeated the room.

Next I learned that the "fever" that kept him in bed was really an alcoholic haze through which he was aimlessly drifting, an aftermath of a trip to Cuba with Zelda from which he had just returned and which, he said, he had handled with drunken disorder. Guilt-ridden and upset that the "holiday" was a fizzle, he tried to make things right with Zelda by mail. He wrote a loving note to her: ". . . You were a peach throughout the whole trip and there isn't a minute of it when I don't think of you with all the old tenderness . . . ." He went on to praise her consideration in relation to his own deplorable behavior.

As I typed the letter, I was deeply moved. It fit my

notions of true romance and I was caught up in the drama of their love and separation.

This was early in May, and though I was still a new employee, Scott talked readily to me about how difficult it was for him to be with Zelda now. When they were together, she seemed better able to cope with him than he with her. She had the security of her treatment and of her hospital, and had no need to stay within the real world; she had an escape hatch. One symptom of her illness was the range of her behavioral extremes. In her normal periods, he said, she was so lucid that when he visited she could make him seem like the patient.

I listened to the confidences, quietly entranced. He was aware that it would never be good for them again. Yet, he could not divorce himself from the haunting remembrance of their youth. Of course, he did not know that their 1939 Cuban vacation would be the last time they would see each other.

■　　■　　■

He wanted me to be unobtrusively on hand for him. I separated the personal from the business mail. I paid the bills and kept the checkbook in balance. When we needed foodstuffs or cigarettes, I phoned the market at Ventura and Sepulveda where he had a charge account, and placed an order. Some days, I picked up the groceries on the way in. For a short time, he had no domestic help so I would order canned soup—turtle and black bean were his favorites. He also liked Smithfield's deviled ham which he ate right out of the tin, or bacon and eggs—food that I could fix for him. The cigarettes that he chain-smoked were filtered Raleighs. He ordered the gin—Gordon's—secretly, and managed to have it

delivered from the small convenience market at the foot
of Amestoy Avenue when I wasn't around. It was part of
his deceptive game of "not drinking."

He tried to write something every day—notes for a
chapter, for a character. He had to feel he was working.
With a knife-sharpened, blunt-edged pencil, he
determinedly put words on paper—some meaningful,
some not. There were days when I arrived and he was
not ready. I waited around. I learned to be patient. I
would walk out into the garden, landscaped with beds
of rose bushes. A plant of small pinks climbed up a
lattice to the upper veranda which was just outside
Scott's bedroom. It was such a peaceful country house.
On fair days, I would sit on the grass and enjoy the sun,
or leaf through a newspaper. After awhile, Scott would
come out wearing a terry cloth bathrobe over a sweater,
over pajamas. We'd stroll about, then go in for some
lunch.

A few weeks after I came on the job, we hired a
cook, Erleen Smith, a handsome woman of good cheer
and incredible kitchen talent. She would prepare lunch.
Most of her effort was wasted on Scott whose appetite
was small, but she could always entice him with
something sweet, especially a delicacy like custard with
its carmelized sugar; he would eat it all, lavishing praise
with every spoonful.

He might then go upstairs and fish out an
unfinished story to see whether it was worth rescuing.
These were low-key days, but neither black nor
depressed. He seemed to need the quiet to find his way.
Ultimately, whatever he wanted to write would land on
paper. The lull gave me time to observe his habits, to

learn that drink did not make him ugly or abusive—at least not to me. Part of the delay in getting down to real work was procrastination and part was just physical exhaustion.

For well over a month, he talked about his new book, each time swearing me to secrecy. All I knew was that the hero would be based on Irving Thalberg, the brilliant MGM executive who had died in 1936 at the age of thirty-seven, after a meteoric rise to the top of Hollywood's most glamorous industry.

■   ■   ■

On one of Scott's restless days when he had more difficulty than usual getting started, it occurred to him that a bed desk would simplify his problem. Could I find a handyman who would build this simple piece of furniture—two sides attached to a top board that would fit across his double bed, wide and deep enough to accommodate his legal-sized worksheets? I would try. We took measurements. Scott held the tape at one end, I at the other. We decided on the length, width and height. Then, using the yellow pages, I found a fix-it shop on Cahuenga Boulevard. I drove to the shop owned by a nice old carpenter in Hollywood, described the function of the piece, and gave him the dimensions. He constructed the desk in a couple of hours and loaded it in my car. I took it back to Encino and up the stairs to Scott's room.

He was pleased with his new toy. We set it up on the bed and it fit perfectly. He went into a small, adjacent workroom, rarely used, where he kept his papers and notebooks. He removed charts and notes that

were tacked on the walls and laid them out on the new
desk in piles. That small effort sapped his energy. He
went back to bed and we spent some time reading out
loud—Ecclesiastes and Keats. I read. He recited. He grew
tearful at the beauty of the poetry and we stopped. I left
him to rest.

■　　■　　■

Still the writing did not begin in earnest. Instead Scott
continued to do preliminary plotting. From the bits and
pieces that I typed, and that he often supplemented with
talk, I began to understand that the novel would tell the
story of the inner structure and conflict of power in the
film studio hierarchy. The hero, a man of unusual
artistic and managerial skills, would in some way
become victimized by his unscrupulous counterparts.

I was fascinated by the possibilities and could
barely wait to see how he would begin. But it was
awhile before that happened. Instead he wrote letters.
His concern for family and friends was often obsessive.
Not only for the problem he read into each new
situation, but for the genuine caring. Yet, he
complained that if it weren't for all the interruptions, he
would be farther along with his work. Distance and
separation did not keep Scottie and Zelda from being
perpetual time stealers. He could neither deny nor
ignore a request from either of them. Nor did he want
to.

In June, 1939, at the end of Scottie's school
semester, her appendix acted up. He made an
appointment with his doctor in Baltimore where he
wanted Scottie to go for a confirming diagnosis. He

involved Zelda in the plans. If surgery was necessary, he wanted Scottie to have it in Asheville so that Zelda could be close by. Everything ultimately worked out well, but it took letters and phone calls and energy. Certainly his concern in this instance was legitimate, but there were other times when requests were minor—a new dress, extra money, permission for Zelda to visit her family. A simple yes or no might have sufficed but his letters were never simple. He was the family control point. He made the rules. While they inevitably got what they wanted or needed, Scott repeatedly stressed the degree of sacrifice it took to answer those needs. And the fact is that he was paying out money that was no longer coming in steadily. Drunk or sober, ill or well, he was the one to balance the budget. He was the one to make the final decision.

He played his roles as father and husband with authority. Other times he played invalid, and wrote of temperatures or T.B. flareups which were designed to arouse more concern for his welfare than an admission of alcoholism might have. All this creative correspondence took almost as much time and effort as developing a story line.

Yet, Scott was a writer—always. That's all he ever wanted to be. His hope was to attain a measure of immortality in the literary world and that stubborn objective repeated itself throughout his lifetime.

By 1940, he wrote to Max Perkins, his editor: "I wish I was in print. It will be odd a year or so from now when Scottie assures her friends I was an author and finds no books procurable . . . . I know the next move must come from me. I have not lost faith. People will buy my next book and I hope I shan't again make the many mistakes of *Tender*."

■   ■   ■

The first time I saw Sheilah Graham was about a week after I was hired. She arrived late one afternoon, breathless, blond and smiling brightly as she stood in the doorway of Scott's room. I had no idea who she was. Scott introduced us—me as his new secretary, Sheilah as a friend who had just returned from a trip. He then told her he had a little more work and would be with her in a few minutes. She said she would wait in the guest room, across a small hallway to the right of the staircase. When she left the room, Scott said that she was a Hollywood columnist and a frequent visitor.

I commented that she was very pretty. I didn't immediately grasp that she was the woman in Scott's west coast life. I was still caught up in the pathos of Zelda's illness.

Sheilah was a younger, English version of Hedda Hopper and Louella Parsons, the duennas of the film gossip scene. She had her own residence in Hollywood, but she and Scott saw each other daily. She had to attend almost all new films, and when Scott felt up to it, he drove into town to join her. Otherwise, she came out to the valley. Weekends were usually spent together in Encino.

Given today's mores, it's hard to believe the precautions they took to avoid the tag of "living together." Of course, Scott was officially married and he and Sheilah needed space for their separate work. Yet it seemed odd that Sheilah, who made her living reporting other people's indiscretions, was an "item" herself. By the double standard of the times, an open liaison was not socially acceptable—even in promiscuous Hollywood.

At first, I felt awkward and in the way—a witness to a clandestine affair. I hadn't read her column but learned that she represented N.A.N.A. I didn't know that N.A.N.A. stood for North American Newspaper Alliance, a syndicate that distributed her columns to many newspapers. Instead, I associated the initials with Zola's *Nana* which conjured up a picture of a "loose woman."

If Sheilah arrived while Scott was still at work, she would come in, kiss him and go off to another part of the house until he was available. Other days, he would excuse me and I would go downstairs to type. If there was no urgent need for copy, I would go home.

The change that came over Scott when Sheilah walked into the room held me spellbound. He could be several men—a romantic, tubercular poet as he lay back wan and wasted and softly said, "Hello, Sheelo," or the instantly nervous, responsive lover unable to wait another minute, or the preoccupied writer, or the taunting alcoholic.

Having lived a family-sheltered life, my knowledge of illicit romance came from novels, films, and fantasy. *Back Street* and *The Way of All Flesh* had left strong impressions. Had I been older, I might have been more cynical and less intrigued by what was going on: yet it was impossible not to be caught up in the ongoing drama as it unfolded.

Sheilah had run out of sympathy with Scott's

drinking and there were some wild exchanges between them. When alcohol bedeviled him, her patience was tried to the extreme. Sometimes she would storm out, other times threaten a permanent break, but Scott was not easily intimidated. No one could *order* him to stop—he would stop when he wanted to. Then came a particularly bad binge when he threatened to kill either himself or her. She left the house in fear and rage.

When he quickly came back to reason, he tried to make peace. Phone calls and flowers went unanswered and unacknowledged. Provoke and repent was his pattern, yet he did not want to lose her. He decided to reach her through me. He dictated a letter to her as if I had written it saying that "Mr. Fitzgerald" was appalled at his behavior, would not bother her again, and would even leave Hollywood if it would help her. He had me sign and mail it. He followed the letter with a lavish gift of flowers and then sent me to visit her to determine her mood.

I agreed to act as his messenger because he was genuinely upset. I stopped by her apartment on my way home and saw that the flowers—a dozen red roses—were arranged in a vase. But Sheilah was adamant. She would never go back to him. He was killing himself with drink and she did not want to stand by and watch, nor did she want to be subjected to his taunts and threats.

When I reported the results of the visit to Scott, he was thoughtful. Then the novelist in him took over to right the romance. The fact that Sheilah kept the flowers was a good sign. She must still have some feelings for him, as, indeed, he had for her. He knew that he had to stop drinking and get back to work. He would show her that he could. And she would return. His plan worked. Sheilah relented. If she wanted to, Sheilah could have found a less complicated lover. She was a popular, lively young woman. But she had been around enough to know that a sober Scott could be gallant and loving, and willing to share his knowledge which Sheilah not only respected but needed. She had lived her life by her wits with only a smattering of education. Scott had undertaken to help her make up for that. Once exposed to the glimmer of Scott's mind, it was hard for her to consider a less luminous man.

■　　■　　■

Scott made continuous stabs at controlling his alcoholism by substituting quantities of Coca Cola and cigarettes. He ate lightly, but enjoyed going into the kitchen to mix up batches of fudge. He'd shuffle around, opening cupboards, mumbling "where's the cocoa, where's the sugar?"

Years later, I learned that the symptoms of hypoglycemia (chronic fatigue, insomnia, depression and pallor) pointed to Fitzgerald as a classic example of the disease. If Scott had such a condition (undiagnosed in his lifetime), it helps to explain the ability to give up drinking and to substitute sugar stimuli once he made up his mind to follow that course. If he could have been treated for low blood sugar, would the pattern of his life have been different?

At least, one need not speculate on his head full of stories and his work ethic. When they came together, he spun a sweet tale. Now and again he would ask me to read a page he had written out loud so he could listen to it for cadence. How it sounded was as important as the sight of the words on paper, as if a blind person had to hear it and a deaf one to read it. He would on occasion change a word here and there, seemingly insignificant, but important to him. Other times, he would ask me to leave the copy with him so he could rearrange it, particularly when it came to the opening of the novel and the language of Cecilia, the narrator. She was a child of Hollywood who was educated in eastern schools. She had to be someone who could communicate with and appeal to readers such as his daughter, Scottie.

■   ■   ■

By early fall of 1939, Scott managed to dispatch a treatment of *Stahr* (his working title for the novel) to Kenneth Littauer, editor of *Collier's Magazine*, in the hope that he would be interested in serializing it. Though Scott had every intention of going ahead with the book whether or not the magazine wanted it, it would be easier for him to work if he had a sizeable chunk of advance money that would remove the financial pressure. Littauer rejected the treatment, calling it "cryptic." He could not envision its development, which implied that he didn't think Fitzgerald knew where he was going with it. Scott was furious at this attack against his professionalism. He paced up and down, sputtering expletives; he phoned Littauer one noon and lashed out at him. I was sure he would have a stroke. But once rid of the furies, he calmed down and dictated a telegram: "No hard feelings. There never has been an editor with pants on since George Lorimer." But there were hard feelings that never went away.

In this same period of rejection, his long-time friend and New York agent, Harold Ober, drew the line and refused Scott another loan. Scott was more hurt than angry. Why now? Ober knew how scrupulous he was about repaying debts even though it sometimes took a long time. He didn't need moralizing and judgment from Ober, he said. He needed support. He judged himself harshly enough. There was no attempt at reconciliation. He severed his relationship with Ober and drew on his own inner resources. If he harbored despair, it was private. If he was weary, it was due to the heavy load he carried. But he would not bow to critics who called him incompetent and irresponsible.

In Ober's defense—if any is needed—he continued to offer help where he thought it would do the most good. To Scottie. The Obers adored her and provided her with a home away from home, a safe harbor. They continued to be her "guardian angels" for as long as she needed them.

■　　■　　■

One morning, when I drove up to the house in Encino, I found a man peering quizzically into the trash barrels filled with empty bottles. "May I help you?" I asked. He looked up and I recognized him from his films as Everett Horton. I had not seen him before because he had been away on tour with a comedy called *Springtime for Henry*, a play he made famous. He shook his head. "Looks like a case of the d.t.'s," he commented. I smiled non-committally and went into the house.

I thought it amusing to find Horton out there with the trash and told Scott about it. He was bothered. He didn't want anyone snooping around—not even Horton.

Scott paid his rent, and he felt that entitled him to privacy. Immediately, he devised a way to outwit the landlord. The next time I went to market, I was to pick up some burlap sacks—the kind potatoes came in—and bring them to the house. Hereafter, filling the bags with the empty bottles and disposing of them became another of my duties.

It was not a task I cherished, and I don't know why I carried it out so dramatically, except that I didn't want to take the sacks home. The less my parents knew about this, the better. So I made a weekly excursion through Sepulveda Canyon—there was no freeway then, only brushy terrain—pulled up by the side of a ravine, waited until the traffic had passed, looked about furtively and quickly tossed the sacks over the hill. After a few such trips, I told him that he would probably be punished in his afterlife by having to fill all those bottles with boats. He chuckled and later adapted the idea for "Pat Hobby's College Days," a story which began: "The afternoon was dark. The walls of Topanga Canyon rose sheer on either side. Get rid of it she must. The clank clank in the back seat frightened her. Evylyn did not like the business at all. It was not what she came out here to do. Then she thought of Mr. Hobby. He believed in her, trusted her—and she was doing this for him."

■   ■   ■

Scott was a loner at this time of his life as well as a private drinker. Only once that I know of did he leave the house at night for an alcoholic excursion. I found out about it early the next morning when I received a phone call to come and pick him up at the Georgia

Street Receiving Hospital in downtown Los Angeles. I was alarmed and drove down at a frantic speed. When I arrived, he was waiting in an anteroom, ashen and embarrassed. We rode back to Encino with very little said. I asked about his car. It was home. He had called a cab to take him to a bar on Santa Monica Boulevard in Hollywood. He was reticent about providing other details. He guessed he'd had too much to drink, and got unruly. I didn't press him further. This was clearly a depth he had not wanted to plumb. It did not happen again.

But the drinking did not stop and I was at a loss to understand his indulgence. Then one Monday, I was greeted at the door by a nurse. This was a surprise. She was an attractive, dark-haired woman who introduced herself simply as Jean. She explained that it had been a rough weekend. Scott's doctor had brought her in to oversee the drying out procedure. This was a new turn. I went up to Scott's room. He looked drained. He quietly said that he probably wouldn't be able to work, but would I stay around.

The nursing continued for at least a couple of weeks. Jean became protective of her patient, and he seemed to enjoy the attention. She was solicitous, available and handsomely paid for her R.N. services. Sheilah and Jean were antagonists. Suspicion was in the air as Jean tried to set up professional boundaries. She was there around the clock, and Sheilah had visiting hours. Jean would often take me aside to tell me that Scott was fine until Sheilah came to visit. I wasn't sure what was happening. Was the presence of Sheilah making him feel guilty about Zelda? I didn't know.

Once again, I stood by, but was aware that Jean was playing on Scott's vulnerability. He was always attentive to her and it seemed to me she had an eye on him. She was divorced and was raising a daughter by herself, which aroused Scott's sympathy.

Scott wanted to do something special for the child. He prevailed upon Sheilah to arrange a studio visit and take the little girl on a set to meet a star. Sheilah obliged. The studio was Warner Brothers, where Bette Davis was shooting *Elizabeth and Essex* with Errol Flynn. In full regalia, she posed for a photo with the youngster who was awestruck and forever grateful to Fitzgerald.

If Jean had an expectation that she might become a permanent fixture, employed or otherwise, and I sensed early on that she wanted to, it was shortlived. When the combination of drying out and paying the nursing bills made Scott aware that the cost had made a sizeable dent in his financial support system, Jean's services were dispensed with.

A shortage of funds invariably brought Scott back into the real world. For all the wallowing in this homemade wasteland, his inherent good sense took over. He was a writer who needed to write. If he neglected that need, he would be nothing and he had not yet reached that point. He may have despaired at his declining readership, but he did not doubt his ability to make his talent work for him. In the previous eighteen months at MGM, he had earned over $85,000, but most of it went to pay Zelda's hospital, Scottie's Vassar tuition and debts to friends. There was only one way up.

It was Maxwell Perkins, the brilliant editor, who

gave Scott the thrust he needed. Ever encouraging, ever a friend, unwaveringly loyal, familiar with the angst that besieges writers, he knew his prodigal Scott well. Scott had sent him a copy of the *Stahr* outline, too. And when *Collier's* rejected the submission, Perkins, instantly sensitive to the effect this might have on Scott's morale, wired him encouragement. He praised the concept of the novel and the new approach to the Hollywood theme. Unsolicited, he promised Scott a small loan of $250 to start with and another thousand by the first of the year.

Scott had approval from Max who had seen him through many dark hours, and who understood him best. He got up out of bed. He became the feisty boxer who clenched his fist and muttered mild obscenities at all agents whom he classified as "sons o' bitches." He would show them. He would win this one.

He began to sort the notes that had been accumulating. He became transformed. The contrast was extraordinary—like watching an athlete who had let himself go to fat decide that he was going to make a comeback. As though starting a rigid exercise program, he made charts of segments of the book and planned how long each segment would be. He divided the segments into episodes and the episodes into chapters. Assorted jottings and anecdotes were assigned to specific areas. Stray bits of description fell into place. He wrote character profiles so that he knew who his people were, what roles they played in the film studio pageant—antagonistic producers, writers, labor leaders. He might make two or three starts before he even considered that he was ready for a "first" draft.

What amazed me was how intensely Scott emerged

from the disarray of the past weeks into a routine that revealed him as a methodical, meticulous craftsman. He was as orderly as an accountant whose facts and figures balance his vision.

But he was also animated and he sparked the air with excitement. It was my first exposure to this new kind of energy. Sometimes the high lasted only a couple of hours. He wrote in his large, uneven hand on oversized paper as many as twelve pages a day—his day, which could begin in the middle of a sleepless night and be picked up again the next morning after a nap. He rarely kept at writing for more than a few hours at a time, maybe three or four at most.

I would triple-space a first copy. He would correct it and I would then give him a fresh double-spaced draft. I didn't mind the re-typing because I was so impressed by the changes and by his ability to be so objective about his work. If one of the characters bothered him, he poked and prodded and analyzed until the person came into focus—much like a sculptor adding a bit of clay, digging out another bit, tearing down and rebuilding until the form was defined. This fearless attack on his manuscript made a lasting impression on me. He was his own best editor.

There were constant alterations in plot sequences. From his notebooks, he drew pet phrases, names, ideas. Like the parts of a jigsaw puzzle, he placed and replaced them until they fit. He knew where he was going, what he would keep and what he might toss out later.

He played with names for the characters. Thalia (the heroine) and Bradogue (the villain) were changed to Kathleen and Brady. He liked the sound of Kathleen. As

for Brady, loosely based on L.B. Mayer, the naming was
purposely Irish. It was a time when Hitler dominated
the news and Scott avoided making the villain Jewish.
He said he had, on occasion, been rebuked for his
portrait of "small, fat and disloyal" Meyer Wolfsheim in
Gatsby. Scott was stung by the criticism which he
considered unfair. Wolfsheim was a character whose
behavior fulfilled a function in the story and had
nothing to do with race or religion. He was a gangster
who happened to be Jewish. But sensitivities were
running high in this period and Scott did not want to
have any link with prejudice or anti-semitism.

Yet when he was in a devilishly alcoholic state, he
was quick to tell me that Sheilah was "part" Jewish,
that Jean, the nurse, was "part" Indian, as if it were
some secret that would bring me over to his side against
them. He knew that I was Jewish, but I was his secretary
and confidante and had given him no cause for name-
calling. Later in the year, he made a big to-do about
giving me time off to observe Yom Kippur. He wrote to
Scottie that I was going to atone for *his* sins. I wasn't
that religious, I kiddingly told him.

■   ■   ■

When he wanted to talk his thoughts out, he would call
"Françoise." That affectionate translation of my name
meant for me to stop typing and ignore the fact that he
had told me he wanted to see whatever I was working on
immediately. I would go to his room, sit down and he
would go into his recitation. For instance, this is how he
envisioned Monroe Stahr, the "tycoon." He was a man
of dimension—a man you could respect even if you were

at odds with him. Stahr had grown out of the jungle over which he presided, yet he did not carry a club. His aggressiveness was understated. Because he had climbed the ladder successfully, he believed that all others had the same chance, that the day of individual success was still possible. He was suspicious of unions and didn't see why writers needed a guild. He was good to his writers and expected loyalty in return. He was benevolent but he was wily, too, and often put several writers to work on the same script making sure each was unaware of the others' assignment. In the end, he would use the better treatment and would deal with the objections of the ones who lost out—later. He would be strong enough to disagree, clever enough to outwit—all in the name of artistry, all in the name of fair play. But it was his game. Compared to other executives, he played with style.

Stahr's obsession was quality—and he used any means to stamp his films with it. He was a pace setter. If he believed in a project, he would put art above profits. He must not be a conventional hero, nor would all his viewpoints command respect. Despite his paternalism, he would ultimately be unable to defeat the unions. He would indeed be "The Last of the Tycoons"—a title Scott considered for awhile. Stahr had an innate shrewdness but was not as shrewd as the moguls who invariably took advantage of him when he was away from the studio, who did not have the courage to confront him with their scheming, who would have destroyed him if he had not died first.

I listened raptly as Stahr came alive. No matter how Scott might ultimately maneuver him through the story, the core of the man would remain. It was exhilarating to hear Scott talk about his characters with such intensity, to see how well he knew them. It was like a dramatic reading. He would watch for a response. I didn't have to say much. If I raised an eyebrow or nodded my head, he wanted to know why. He never dismissed a reaction. Nor did he need constant affirmation. He made you feel your input was important. You were the ultimate reader.

Kathleen was not as easy to delineate. She was more elusive, more fragmented—as if he were cautious about revealing her. As he progressed with the book, she grew into it, became less imagined, more believable. She mirrored Scott's relationship with Sheilah, which had developed into a comfortable, trusting alliance. Initially, Stahr was attracted to Kathleen because her pastel beauty reminded him of his late wife. Yet there was a magnetic pull that was stronger than the memory Stahr carried around. Kathleen was different. She was not a Hollywood woman. She was not dependent on him and both Stahr and Scott were fascinated by the possibilities of dealing with a strong but warmly beautiful heroine.

Scott toyed with the epilogue. Three youngsters might be hiking in the mountains and would accidentally come upon the partial wreckage of the plane in which Stahr had crashed. They might find souvenirs, a briefcase, jewelry, maybe some money. What they pick out of the rubble brings their individual character traits into perspective and indicates the paths they might follow in the future. The mechanics of how they would get to this isolated region to make it plausible, and whether there would be a leader among them for good or for evil were unresolved, but he intended to explore the possibilities. He was challenged and intrigued by the symbolism, by the morality-play aspect of such an ending.

These were stimulating hours—lessons for me in building a story, tearing it down, redoing it. Scott was never discouraged at having to start over. Talking didn't seem to affect the freshness of the writing, but the discussions remained private and I was still on my honor not to share them with the outside world.

■   ■   ■

A few weeks of daily focus on *Stahr* put Scott on track, so that by September, 1939, when he had to go on a writing detour, he was able to lay the novel away without suffering. Besides, there was no choice. Money problems were a nag that wouldn't disappear. There never was a time when he could just hole up in a room and write the book to the finish. He was unable to get ahead of monthly family financial committments even though his own living expenses were modest. He drove a used '37 Ford convertible and his few indulgences were books and records. Yet the threat of going into debt was constant.

What he needed was a small but steady income, and a fictional character named Pat Hobby came to the rescue. Pat was a down-at-the-heels, crafty, immoral Hollywood hanger-on who "knew where the body was buried" as the saying went, and who would do anything for money. Always a mediocre writer, he was left over from the days when screenwriting was elementary, and he was kept on the studio payroll so he could be kept off somebody's back. Scott envisioned him as a prototype for a series of short stories that would almost write themselves and would serve as a punching bag for his own frustrations. Certainly Pat was not Scott, nor did Scott, even in his lowest moments, ever consider himself a hack. But the irony of having Pat embody Scott's mercurial mood and financial instability was appealing.

The Pat Hobby stories didn't need much planning. Pat had no sense of right and wrong and Scott didn't hold back. The more he put his corrupt anti-hero through the paces of Hollywood chicanery, the more attached to him he became. He ran Pat through a series of cunning plots and turned out devilish, anecdotal shorts with astonishing speed—sometimes in a night, or over a weekend—always written out in longhand. A draft would be on my desk when I came to work.

The target was *Esquire*, a comparatively new magazine that published the leading writers of the day— George Jean Nathan, Hemingway, Dos Passos. The format included men's high fashion, racy cartoons and Varga pinup girls. It was also open to new writing and satire rather than the romances and adventures that appeared in the *Saturday Evening Post* and *Collier's*.

Since his split with Harold Ober, Fitzgerald had no agent and decided to handle his own stories. He fell into the role of wheeler-dealer with fervor. Editor Arnold Gingrich would have had an easier time dealing with an agent than with the author who would send off a story and badger for immediate response and a request that payment be wired to his Bank of America account in

Culver City. Before beginning another Pat antic, he would make innumerable minor changes. I would put the corrections in an envelope and race through the valley to the main Los Angeles airport, then located in Burbank, to post the story changes. Scott did not trust the local post office with airmail. He was more than anxious, as these short pieces were his only new work appearing in print and he wanted them to be up to Fitzgerald standard.

When Gingrich seemed willing to buy as many pieces as Scott turned out, he began to think that *Esquire* was "stealing" them. He asked for a raise. Gingrich was unable to pay it. Hot and angry words passed between them and almost put an end to Pat Hobby. But Gingrich had the generosity to make the first conciliatory gesture. A telegram arrived:

> DEAR SCOTT WE MENNONITES COOL DOWN
> QUICKER THAN YOU FIGHTING IRISH SO SUGGEST
> YOU DONT ANSWER THIS UNTIL TOMORROW BUT
> AFTER YOU HUNG UP I REALIZED THAT IF MY
> UNFORTUNATE CHOICE OF WORDS IN MY WIRE
> HURT YOU HALF AS MUCH AS YOUR LAST SPOKEN
> WORDS HURT ME THEN IT IS INEFFABLY SILLY FOR
> TWO ADULTS TO FIGHT A MUTUALLY UNWANTED
> WAR OVER A RELATIVELY SMALL AMOUNT OF
> MONEY AFTER SIX YEARS OF FRIENDLY AND
> PEACEFUL GIVE AND TAKE IN WHICH MUTUAL
> UNDERSTANDING AND FORBEARANCE HAS
> SMOOTHLY OILED THE EXCHANGE OF SOME
> SEVENTY FIVE THOUSAND WORDS AND SEVENTY
> FIVE HUNDRED DOLLARS WITHOUT DAMAGE TO
> FRIENDSHIP WHICH LATTER COMMODITY IS TO ME
> AT LEAST A MORE PRECIOUS CURRENCY THAN
> CASH . . . .

The message went on to assure Scott that Gingrich could be counted on. Scott found his sincerity irresistible.

In the end, Pat the hack served his master well, and with the encouragement from Gingrich (who later compiled the stories into a book) he endures as a comic personality along with Scott's more carefully crafted romantic types.

■   ■   ■

We had two brief studio experiences. Both were taken to plug the gaping financial hole and both were insignificant.

The first was a one-week assignment in late August, 1939, at the Samuel Goldwyn Studios in Hollywood. The weather was hot and muggy, and Scott came prepared with a briefcase full of Coca Colas. The film, *Raffles*, was well into production and was about a debonair detective. It starred David Niven and Olivia de Havilland. Scott was hired to re-write some of the static, romantic dialogue. It had to be done in a week because Niven had been called to duty by the British Armed Forces. The war was on in Europe and this would be his last film for the duration.

We were given a quiet corner on the set with lights, cameras and action going on around us, and were both smitten by Niven—a man of extraordinary charm—lean, handsome, elegant. He smiled at me in passing, and I dissolved. Scott, too, could barely conceal his hero-worship and identified with the real-life role Niven was about to play. Thus inspired, he wrote the additional lines of dialogue to everyone's satisfaction, for the sum of $1,200.

When the session was over, Scott drove me home. My brother Morton, a college student, was at the door when we arrived and I introduced them. They chatted. Morton recalls that Fitzgerald said that Niven felt he would not live through the war. Fitzgerald seemed caught up in the drama of a hero gallantly going off to his death.

The second studio stint came about a year later. Scott really wanted to stay with his novel, but could not afford to turn down the money. Besides, Darryl Zanuck, the head of 20th Century-Fox, wanted Scott to work on adapting an Emlyn Williams play, *The Light of Heart*, for the screen.

I rather looked forward to getting inside the magical gates. Tyrone Power was one of their big stars. Perhaps I would run into him on the lot.

Scott was now living on Laurel Avenue and my family had moved to Westwood, so it was easy for me to hop a bus to the studio. We would meet at the Writers' Building, a group of cottages in mock English country architecture that circled a little garden. Once again, Scott would arrive with a briefcase of Cokes to help him get through the day. We joked about selling the idea of Coke in a briefcase to the Coca-Cola company.

Scott dictated ideas for treating the play. I typed up the notes in a small adjoining office. When he had gone as far as he could, the partial treatment was sent to the front office and we waited for a call from Zanuck. It took days. In the meantime, Scott caught up with his correspondence. A call finally came through; a meeting was set up for eleven o'clock at night. Zanuck would be having a massage and could discuss the project while he was being pounded. I went home and so did Scott. He would return later.

At seven the next morning, I was awakened by a telegram:

> HIGHLY SUCCESSFUL CONFERENCE FROM ELEVEN
> TO ONE A.M. PLEASE BE AT OFFICE BY TEN-TWENTY
> TO HOLD FORTH BUT DON'T PHONE ME UNLESS
> HEADQUARTERS CALL. A THOUSAND WILD STORMY
> KISSES [SIGNED] TYRONE.

I went to the studio and took up my post. When Scott arrived he did some dictating. I typed his notes, but the actual screenplay typing was turned over to the studio secretarial pool. As we waited for a reaction from the upper echelon, Scott often took his shoes off to

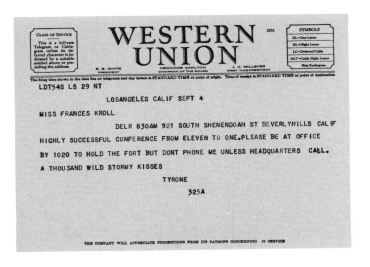

relieve the "squeeze." Ultimately, the treatment was
rejected as too "down-beat." It all came to nothing and I
never did get to see "Tyrone."

■   ■   ■

Trying to anticipate a day's routine was like trying to
guess the weather. Fair or not, there was always a bit of
staging.

I arrived about ten one morning. There was a note
on my desk along with papers full of markings and
arrows. The note read:

> Dear François: This is a development of this earlier
> chart. It will still just go on one big page—that is
> it will if the first column (The English stuff) will.
> Notice it's a little different in categories. Am
> sleeping.

The instructions referred to the reading lists Scott was preparing for the education of Sheilah Graham. It was busywork for me and kept Scott pushing a pencil while the novel simmered. The lists ultimately became the survey course that Sheilah later called her "College of One," a study plan Scott devised in history, literature and the arts. It was indeed a master class and discussions of her "lessons" gave a Pygmalion-like dimension to their relationship.

I typed the individual courses on legal-sized paper set in the machine horizontally. This particular list was Drama and Poetry from Shakespeare to Synge to Shaw, supplemented with contemporary poetry and popular history—Wells' *Outline of History* and Van Loon's *The Arts*.

By the time I had the paper in the typewriter, Scott appeared in bathrobe, a bit disheveled, finished with sleeping. He explained that he woke in the night and worked on the lists. He thought he would be tired in the morning but he now felt fine and had a few more corrections. Could he make them before I got started?

I groaned.

He was amused. I should be glad that he was making the changes before rather than after the typing was done.

I agreed and bowed low in mock gratitude. It was not my favorite chore, but I made use of the labor to learn from it and to supplement my own spotty reading.

Some days, he would send me off to used book stores to look for copies of the titles on the reading list. In 1939, Sixth Street in downtown Los Angeles was book row. Shop after shop—the Argonaut, The Curio,

Holmes Book Company—was filled to the dark rafters. They overflowed to outdoor open stalls where one could get real bargains. I picked up a small, specially bound edition of Flaubert's *Three Tales* for fifty cents. I found *Alice in Wonderland* with Tenniel illustrations and a copy of Renan's *Life of Jesus* for under two dollars. After several successful book searches, I developed a warm spot for downtown Los Angeles.

While on these excursions, I would stop in at the main branch of the public library on Fifth Street to scan (at Scott's request) the bound volumes of old newspapers for information on Irving Thalberg, Louis B. Mayer or any hard news relating to MGM and local labor union leaders. There were no instant copy machines in those days, so I would write down whatever was pertinent in shorthand and type up the notes when I returned.

On occasion Scott, feeling good, would take an afternoon off and drive himself down for a book hunt. There was a young man at The Holmes Book Company named Bob Bennett who helped him find good secondhand copies of Shaw's *The Intelligent Woman's Guide to Socialism* and Chapman's *Homer*. Scott was never a casual customer and drew out people, got them to talk about themselves. When Bennett mentioned that he wrote poetry, Scott asked to read the verses.

"He gave me some very helpful lines and told me the things he liked," said Bennett. "Sometimes, we would have coffee next door—at Mackie's. He was concerned about *Tender Is The Night* and wondered how it would rank with *Grapes of Wrath*. He was a little exasperated with Steinbeck for having written something so popular."

From F Scott Fitzgerald
to Frances Kroll
at the start of an
ambitious enterprise.

With Mutual Good
Wishes

"F Scott Fitzgerald
(or did I say that
before — anyhow with
esteem + affection)

On February 12, 1940, he bought and gave Bennett an inscribed copy of *Tender*. In fact, during the course of 1939-40 he bought up whatever copies of his works were available around town. When his next royalty statement came through from Charles Scribner's Sons, the handful of sales proved that the author, himself, was the only purchaser. He told me about it, laughing bitterly.

He gave me three of those precious volumes which I treasured for their inscriptions: In *The Great Gatsby*, he wrote:

> From F. Scott Fitzgerald to Frances Kroll at the start of an ambitious enterprise.
> With mutual good wishes
> F. Scott Fitzgerald
> (or did I say that before—anyhow with esteem and affection)

In *Taps at Reveille*, he wrote a ditty:

Frances Kroll
She has a soul
   (She claims to know it)
But when young Frances
Does her dances
She don't show it.
   "From the bald headed
man in the front row
      Scott Fitzgerald
      "The Gayieties"
         1939

Frances Kroll
She has a soul
   (She claims to know it)
But when young Frances
Does her dances
   She don't show it.

*from The bald headed
man in the front row
   Scott Fitzgerald
   "The Gayeties"
      1939

For Francis Kroll
in memory of those
Happy years together
on the Riverra which
inspired this book
from her admirer,
F Scott Fitzgerald
1939

In *Tender is the Night*:

For Frances Kroll in memory of those happy years
together on the Rivierra which inspired this book
from her admirer

F. Scott Fitzgerald
1939

For all his scrupulous editing, he never did learn how to
spell very well.

■   ■   ■

There were the afternoons when the valley heat would
settle heavily on the roof of the house making the
upstairs unbearably warm. Scott would amble down to
my "office" which was a shade cooler. I worked in a
guest room off the dining area which contained a bed, a
typewriter, and a large antique table that I used as a
desk.

Scott would grab a cold Coke from the kitchen and
sit on the bed, propping himself up against the
headboard while I typed. After a while, he would start
talking about whatever came into his head. "Bunny"
was a favorite subject. It was Bunny—Edmund Wilson,
whom he had met at Princeton—who most strongly
influenced his political thinking and reading, who had
directed him to Marx and later to Kafka. I had never
read Kafka, I told him. He said I must read *The Trial*
not only for Kafka's brilliant style, but to understand
what was happening to the individual under a
dictatorship. I was unable to find the book in Los
Angeles until years later. By then, I was struck by an
unusual coincidence. *The Trial* was assembled after

Kafka's death by his friend, German novelist Max Brod, and it was Wilson who edited Fitzgerald's last novel after his death. It just seemed an odd footnote to that bit of casual conversation.

Politically, Scott thought of himself as a liberal. He had voted for Roosevelt twice, but he was a passive, theoretical liberal, not an active one. I have a clear picture in mind of him lounging on the bed remarking that he would like to see a workers' revolution happen here, but he didn't want to be part of it. He would prefer to be up in a tower, preferably an ivory one, watching rather than participating. How much of this talk was to work out the union problems he was dealing with in the novel, and how much was what he was seriously thinking, I don't know.

Yet he wrote to Scottie about Marx: "You can neither cut through, nor challenge nor beat the fact that there is an organized movement over the world before which you and I as individuals are less than the dust . . . read the terrible chapter in *Das Kapital* on the Working Day and see if you are ever quite the same."

Inevitably, political talk led to "Ernest" whose involvement in causes was very visible, and had been ever since his participation in the Spanish Civil War. His adventures were front page news. Scott had an explanation of his friend's public courtship of danger— that he had to prove himself to himself. Scott was bothered by Hemingway's need to constantly play stage center and felt it was beginning to have a negative effect on his writing. In his own fantasy life, Scott, too, was a crusader, a knight errant, a hero. He had his own kind of strength. But his priorities were different. He neither would nor could leave his wife and child and "go off to the wars" or to the wilds of Africa. On his scale of commitment, prudence held the balance.

When Hemingway sent him an inscribed copy of *For Whom the Bell Tolls*, he wrote a vague, equivocal acknowlegement: "it's a fine novel better than anybody else writing could do." But to editor-father Max Perkins he confided his disenchantment with Ernest's writing—specifically with *The Green Hills of Africa* and *For Whom the Bell Tolls*—at the same time asking "What do you hear from Ernest . . . how does Ernest feel about things?" still caring too much to be able to reject him.

Perkins knew well the differences between the two men and the different kind of men they were. Ernest showed no sensitivity when he expressed public disdain for Scott in "Snows of Kilimanjaro" referring to him as "poor Scott." Scott was hurt and angry and wrote Ernest to lay off him in print at the same time praising the story. Perkins also knew Scott's need to be treated with honest affection, at least for past kindnesses—he did, after all, bring Hemingway to the attention of Perkins. In this period, Hemingway was turning out book after book, yet Scott still wanted to be regarded a favorite on the Scribner roster. Perkins played surrogate father to both men. He went fishing with Hemingway. He loaned Scott money and emotional support. He listened to complaints from each about the other. His compliant nature enabled him to juggle the demands of these two volatile writers while keeping his balance as editor to both.

Scott did not wear the uniform of citizen-at-large as Ernest did, but he was no less aware of the political rumblings and war maneuvers in Europe. In armchair strategy, he hung onto the World War I Maginot Line defense which he thought was indomitable. When Hitler's armies trampled it and goose-stepped into France, Scott was outraged and went back to the drawing board and his war games. He may well have envied Hemingway out in the field with a beautiful correspondent while he did his playing at home. It seemed that Hemingway was often on Scott's mind.

If they could have been less like siblings and more like a couple of politicians who crucify each other in a campaign and then shake hands, they might have continued to communicate. But Hemingway was not a peacemaker. He was as blunt in his evaluation of Scott as he was of Zelda and he was not a man to back off once he had expressed his view. It was a complicated relationship—two opposites attracted to each other's talents—one battering away at any wall that blocked his path to wherever he wanted to go, the other living within the taut walls of stress. Ultimately each destroyed himself.

■   ■   ■

Scott asked a lot of questions about my family, and about Jews and Irish in relation to drinking. Did I know any Jewish alcoholics? There weren't any in my family, I told him. We always had liquor in the house, but I'd never seen my father drink more than a "schnapps" before dinner. Scott wanted me to keep talking so I told him about the Passover feast where Manischewitz was prominent. Even though we were supposed to down four cups at a Seder, the wine never made anyone drunk.

I recalled that my grandfather had done some very limited private distilling of his own using a mixture of raisins, prunes, sugar and alcohol. It was called "med" and was a dessert wine—very heady. As children, we were each given a little taste of it, but I had no recollection of the men in the family sitting around getting bombed.

Why? he wondered.

Probably because they liked to eat more than they liked to drink. They enjoyed their food. We made much of the Sabbath dinner, the Passover feast, the high holidays, the harvest. Each holiday had its own food ritual. Passover was special because it was like a spring cleaning. All the bread and bleached flour had to be tossed. The house was made "kosher" and the pots and pans were scoured. I grew up in the age of the icebox and all food had to be bought fresh—almost daily. Fresh fish and freshly slaughtered chickens were my mother's priorities. This fascinated Fitzgerald.

One Passover, I told Scott, my father went to an extreme to oblige her and brought home a *live* carp. He had bought it at a local fish market where they had huge tanks of fish swimming about. We were all excited, but where would we keep it. It was thrashing its way out of the wet newspaper wrapping. Without delay, mother went to the bathtub, scrubbed it, filled it with fresh water and the fish was given the run of the tub. As we had only one bathroom in our apartment, that meant no baths for us until it was time to start holiday cooking. At that point, my father clobbered the fish over the head with a hammer and dressed it before mother converted it to its *gefüllte* state.

Scott shook his head in disbelief at this fish story. Then a cunning light came into his eyes as he commented that he would never have brought the fish to such a savage end. He would simply have filled the tub with gin and let the fish drink itself into oblivion.

In another of our afternoon chats, Scott wanted to know more about my father—where he came from, what his education had been. I told him that Pop had lived on a farm in Russia and his only education had been the study of the Bible in Hebrew. The Good Book had dictated the pattern of his life and he could still recite long passages from memory. When he was thirteen, he went to Petrograd to become apprentice to a furrier. There he learned his trade. In 1907, the rumblings of discontent with Czarist Russia were strongly felt and at age 16, Pop left for America without knowing a word of English, without a spare ruble. He settled in New York and quickly found work despite the language barrier, or maybe because of it, as most of the other furriers couldn't speak much English either. It was not exactly a rags-to-riches story, but Pop always had confidence in his ability to make a living and to put food on the table. He came to Los Angeles with that same immigrant sense of a new life in a new place and after a rough start, he found his stride.

The story resembled the beginnings of many Hollywood moguls, and Scott said it helped him to put certain pieces into place.

A few days after our talk, Scott sent a gift home. It was a recently published Simon & Schuster edition of the Bible—a combination of the Old and New Testaments in the King James Version. He inscribed it:

For Samuel Kroll
    from a friend and collaborator of his daughter—
hoping that whether or not he agrees with this
modern way of translating Scripture, it may give
him some interest to glance over it

                                    F. Scott Fitzgerald

Encino, 1939

■   ■   ■

Working days continued to be irregular. If Sheilah was
out of town on a film assignment, I would stay on later,
not because there was so much to do, but because Scott
did not like facing the night alone. Once in a frivolous,
tipsy state, he made a grab for me. I pulled away. He was
immediately abashed and said, "I won't do that again. I
wouldn't want to think of Scottie in such a situation."

We continued to have a good working relationship.
Of course, he was a romantic character to me—like an
exiled prince in a period novel. But he was not my
prince. How could he be? He was almost my father's age
and despite good looks and gentle ways, he aroused
compassion rather than passion. There was nothing I
wouldn't do for him because he was considerate, polite,
never ordered me about, and was generous in
acknowledging daily help. Besides, he was the most
intellectually stimulating man I had ever known and I
was, by now, enamored of his style as a writer.

I felt deep affection and empathy as I darted in and
out of his moods. In one of his bleak moments between
drinking and writing, he asked me not to come in for a
couple of days. He mumbled something about revising
an old story. The next day he sent me a letter:

For Samuel Kroll
from a friend
and collaborator of
his daughters —. hoping
that whither or not
he agrees with this
modern way of translating
Scripture, it may give
him some interest to
glance over it

F Scott Fitzgerald

Encino, 1939

Dear François: Haven't felt like writing—or thinking—or anything much. It occurred to me today you may be needing this. Have made it $25.00 because you say you have money from last check to Scottie.
Always Afftly Yrs
Scott.
   Will phone when anything seems to particularly matter.

I was quick to take on his depression and hung
around my house waiting. The money he referred to had
to do with my salary which I took haphazardly,
depending on the state of his bank account. After a
couple of days, I phoned him. How was the story going?
He gave no direct answer, instead asked me to drop by.
When I arrived there was a note on my desk:

> Not writing any story, you must have
> misunderstood on phone. But glad to see you.

Before the end of the day, the darkness had lifted.
Scott wandered into my room to see how I was doing
and gave me something to type.

During productive spurts, after long stretches of
typing and retyping, he would suddenly be filled with
concern for me. I was too young to be spending so much
time with him, he said. What was I doing socially? Did I
go out? Did I have a boyfriend? I did go out. I didn't
have a particular boyfriend. Most "boys" seemed a bit
dull after a day with Scott.

He had his own way of saying "thank you"—like
the time he had preview passes to *Destry Rides Again*, a
western starring James Stewart and Marlene Dietrich.
He was unable to go and insisted that I get on the phone
immediately and round up a date. Luckily, I was able to
reach a friend who was free or Scott might have taken
the matter in hand. Next day I reported catching a
glimpse of glamorous Marlene in the lobby of
Hollywood's Pantages Theatre. She was beautiful
beyond belief. It was exciting to see the *star* in person
even though I didn't think the film was so great. Neither

Not writing any story, you must have misunderstood on phone But glad to see you,

did I appreciate her raspy rendition of "See What the Boys in the Back Room Will Have." The movie later became a minor classic because of Dietrich's offbeat performance. So much for my critique.

What did we do after the movie? Scott wanted to know. We went to a small bar on La Cienega where Dinah Washington, jazz pianist and song stylist, made delicious music. Scott was pleased. He had directed me toward an evening well spent.

■　　　■　　　■

Nothing was simple with Scott Fitzgerald. Mundane tasks became extraordinary. Balancing a checkbook, paying bills, and preparing income taxes turned into a test of nerves.

He had a fear of bureaucratic hassle and repeated instructions over and over to make sure I got everything right. He owed back taxes (less than a thousand dollars) and did not want to draw attention to his new return. I was to be sure to put the name and address on the envelope exactly as it appeared on the tax form—not just Fitzgerald or FSF but F. Scott Fitzgerald—otherwise he might not be properly credited. I assured him that I knew how to address the envelope, but he insisted that I show it to him before mailing it just to be sure.

Even making a dental appointment was a complicated routine. It was not a matter of picking up a phone and setting up a time. First, he would send me a telegram. It would arrive early in the morning—wakeup time.

> TRY TO MAKE DENTIST APPOINTMENT BETWEEN ONE AND FIVE FOR FULL HOUR. TELL HIM IT IS AN EMERGENCY. CALL ME AT NOON. REGARDS SCOTT.

The time on the message indicated that he had phoned it in at 2:30 in the morning. Within a few minutes another message arrived which he had sent at 4 a.m. It read:

> FOLLOWING OTHER TELEGRAM TRY TO MAKE APPOINTMENT AS NEAR 2:30 P.M. AS POSSIBLE STOP DON'T WANT ANYTHING AS LATE AS 5 TO 6 SCOTT.

The dentist, who was a family friend, said he would fit him in.

Scott kept his appointment and before I left the house that evening I wrote him a note:

"I squeezed the oranges, boiled the coffee, laid the eggs, typed the story, put out the cat, started the dogs howling and I'm off to the city. Hope you have a good night's rest. Your devoted secretary, Francoise."

He kept the note for laughs but it didn't change that odd turn of mind that made him worry so about details. In the end, humor provided the delicate balance for both of us.

■　　■　　■

Getting to work was a major problem for me. Though my family generously let me continue to use our Pontiac, it was troublesome for them which bothered me. One day, as I drove along Ventura Boulevard, two cars appeared from out of nowhere and before I knew what hit me, there was a three-way crash. Nobody was hurt, but my vehicle was immobilized. Even though the accident was not my fault, I was terribly upset— primarily because the car was not mine. Not only would it further inconvenience my family, but it would be impossible for me to get to work. Those were not the days of easy rent-a-car facilities. I looked so forlorn that one of the other drivers asked if I needed a lift. He drove me to Encino.

By the time I arrived, Scott was frantic. Why was I so late? When I told him I'd had a car crash, he rushed me into that long living room which we hardly ever used, opened the doors and windows and hovered. He did not offer me a drink to settle me down, but kept asking, are you all right? Do you want to lie down? Should you go to a doctor? I finally convinced him that I was intact but should phone my parents and the insurance company. Of course, of course. He walked me to the phone to be sure I could manage.

It ended up being a week of inconvenience. Erleen, the cook, told me not to worry. She would lend me her big, solid old Buick for going home. On the weekend, Scott suggested that if I drove him to Sheilah's I could keep his Ford until Monday by which time my car would be repaired. It was a generous gesture and I was grateful. We started out. We drove along the highway at an easy pace until I became aware that Scott was staring at the speedometer. "Is something wrong?" I asked. He shook his head "no" so I kept going. After awhile, he asked rather tensely, "Aren't you going a little fast?"

"Only 35 miles an hour."

"Seems faster," he said even though the figures on the dashboard were very clear.

I didn't answer.

"There's a red light ahead," he cautioned.

"I can see it." By now it was apparent that the accident would make my driving forever suspect to him. My dander rose. Did he want to take the wheel? I would pull over and change places. No, no, he said. I kept on driving. No words passed between us. As we came closer to town and it became clear that we would make it without crashing, he lightened up. When we reached La Cienega Boulevard, he broke into a little song: "On La Cienega, there's a five-and-tenega." The tension fell away.

■   ■   ■

The summer of 1939 came before Scott was ready for it. There were no real seasons in his life save working or not working, and he had begun to work—just begun. So when Scottie wrote to ask about vacation plans and to suggest a visit, his reaction bore elements of panic. Yes, he wanted to see her but he anticipated her visit as a homecoming of all her problems. He would rather handle them by letter. She must not think he could stop the clock and take time off for her. This was another invasion of his work time. How would he entertain her? He didn't know many people anymore. He'd have to call Charlie Brackett, a writer-producer friend who had two daughters, and try to get the girls together. Maybe arrange a lunch. She would have to take driving lessons. Now that she was going out with boys who had cars, she ought to be able to drive in case one of the boys had too much to drink.

He went on and on thinking up potential disasters. He never considered that her dating game might be different from that of his generation; that every boy didn't drink; that Scottie and a date were not Zelda and Scott. He barraged her with letters that would have driven a lesser child crazy. If anything proved Scottie's ability to cope, this episode did. He painted a dark, bleak picture of life in Encino. He took protective cover. If the visit turned out badly, she would at least have been forewarned.

As I typed the letters, I wondered why he couldn't just tell her that he had spent a hellish spring recovering from his "Cuban holiday"; that he was just getting into a work routine she would have to respect. What I didn't know was that her two previous visits had been disasters for him. Each time Scott had been drinking and trying to conceal it. He had been nervous, irrational and feared that he might repeat the behavior. He really didn't want to. Instead, he sent up sarcastic warning signals. "Do you want to come out and be my secretary?" he asked. "Let us laugh mirthlessly with a Boris Karloff ring."

Scottie was not put off by his signals. Hollywood was still a very glamorous place and she was able to accept a visit to the coast on her own level. As she recalled her previous vacation when she was fifteen, "It was as close to heaven as you could get to meet Joan Crawford and Clark Gable and Bette Davis and wander through the studio lots watching the movie being made. Everybody, even the celebrities, was terribly nice to me. I suppose I was something of a novelty in the bustling Hollywood of that time, an innocent little square out of a fashionable Eastern boarding school with the perfect manners I'd had drummed into me by my English nanny. One day, impressed by the flashy costumes of the stars, I went out and bought a long chiffon dress studded with rhinestones. Daddy nearly had a fit and made me take it back immediately. In those days, there wasn't any such thing as a youth rebellion among the kids I knew. You did as you were told and that was that."

In the end, Scott agreed to the visit despite his anxiety about planning her activities, about setbacks in his work as a result of her daily presence. Of course he wanted to see her, and of course he loved her deeply. It was himself he could not trust.

Scott and Scottie, as father and daughter, were a puzzle to me. I was not much older than Scottie, who was eighteen—but I came from so different a background, was so integrated into a strong family life and had so much more personal freedom that I couldn't understand all his fears about her. True, he did his fathering by mail, but he set down ground rules that I would have been unable to keep.

It wasn't always that way. As a little girl, Scottie was adored. "I can remember nothing but happiness and delight in his company until the world began to be too much for him when I was about twelve," said Scottie. "Daddy never let me feel the tragedy of mother's illness and I never had a sense of being unloved."

Her warmest memories are of Maryland where they leased a house on an estate called La Paix. It was owned by the Turnbull family who lived in a larger house on the property and Scottie had the daily companionship of their children. "It was like being in a big family . . . and Daddy was right in the midst of things with us."

The love lavished on Scottie from the start by Scott and Zelda remained to blanket her through her teens, with enough residue to last her through maturity.

■　　■　　■

But when Scott headed out to Hollywood in quest of money to settle his debts, leaving fifteen-year-old Scottie behind was very difficult. She gave motivation to his life. She was his future—his continuity. And he overcompensated for his absence with letters that were meant to guide her, control her behavior, and give her a set of values. He did not want her to feel abandoned. Neither did he want her to feel that she could get away with violating his rules just because he wasn't close by. He seemed to use his deep feeling for her as a threat; he loved her and she had better not forget it.

He never wrote down to her. But he was relentless. If the reports from her housemother at school stressed untidiness, he pounced on her and compared her bad habits to Zelda's tendency for disorder. If she neglected math and Latin, which she hated, he got on her back about focusing only on subjects that were easy for her. He acknowledged that she was above average in English, but he expected that of her. The barriers were always up.

In retrospect, Scottie handled adolescence in what now appears to have been a well-adjusted manner. It is to her credit that she had the good sense to ignore what she didn't want to heed and tuck the letters away for future reading rather than toss them out. She couldn't understand why he fussed so and kept reassuring him that she was leading a righteous and sober life.

To her he was always "daddy" first and writer second. When she thought of contemporary writers, she thought of Margaret Mitchell and when he wrote her that he was working on the screenplay of *Gone With the Wind* she was very impressed. She wrote him that she thought it was one of the great masterpieces of all time. His stinging reply was that it was "interesting, surprisingly honest, consistent and workman-like throughout and I felt no contempt for it but only a certain pity for those who considered it the supreme achievement of the human mind."

He was compulsive about Scottie's education and impressed upon her that she would be the *first woman* in the family to try for a college education. She must be prepared to have an independent life with a rod of knowledge up her back to support it. Under all of Scott's parental nagging was a concern for Scottie's future. He was keenly aware of a changing world for women and he wanted his daughter to be ready for that world with education, goals, self-esteem. She must not fritter away her life as so many young women in the twenties had. She must have a respect for ideas. She must have ideas of her own. Scottie might well have found her own way without his prodding but he was not taking chances. Every letter he wrote, every instruction he gave was amplified to penetrate an inner ear just in case she wasn't listening. He more than made up for the distance between them with time, energy and as much remote control as he could exercise.

If, in calm moments, he recognized his excesses, he apologized. Scottie was always "Dearest Pie" and even after interminable written lectures, he mustered enough humor to say, "I send you a bonus of five dollars, not for any reason but simply because a letter without a check will probably seem to you half-filled." There was always "Dearest Love" at the end.

The facet of his stern fathering that I related to and even envied was the push to continue her schooling. I had been a good student in high school, but there was no insistence that I go on to college. Though I valued education, it seemed more important to get a job in those depressed economic times and learn through "practical experience." I would continue to educate myself through reading and supplementary courses at night school. College in the '30s was not an available option or even a consideration for all young women. And just such an option was being pressed on Scottie.

Yet, Scott was so caught up in his ongoing battle to turn his daughter into a serious woman, that he kept forgetting how old she was. She was a teenager and popular with her peers. She says now that she wishes she had not been so frivolous. But if she had been buried in books all the time and if she had been asocial, Scott would have fretted that she wasn't having a good time or that she wasn't attractive to boys. His priorities often got confused and he was inclined toward anxiety no matter what she did. Mail-order authority was undoubtedly frustrating and his words were chosen for emphasis as well as for posterity. As he put it—at *Saturday Evening Post* rates, most of his letters were worth $4,000 and she was getting them for nothing.

The teen years are break-away years. Though Scottie didn't outwardly rebel, there was no way she could have been expected to "yes, daddy" him all the time. On the one hand, he wanted her to have fun—on the other, when she went off for a weekend to have some, he suspected the worst, made frantic phone calls trying to track her down, sent telegrams, imagined illicit behavior and let his own devils run rampant in her direction.

■   ■   ■

By the time Scottie was due to arrive in Los Angeles for her summer vacation, the only impression I had of her was formed from the correspondence I had typed. I thought that she was probably one "fast kid." When I went to the Union Station to pick her up, I looked for a very blond, sexy, brash movie-starlet type. I walked up and down the platform and back into the station peering about for someone who would fit the image. How would I deal with such a young woman? Would she and Scott argue a lot? Would he pit us one against the other? Then I spotted the Fitzgerald face in a new, fresh frame—unspoiled, natural blond hair falling casually to her shoulders. No makeup. She looked small and a little lost as I approached to introduce myself. She broke into an easy smile of relief. She, too, hadn't known whom to expect. We went to collect her luggage and as she looked for her bags, I watched and was impressed by a certain style and poise that were hers quite naturally. I wondered why Scott had been so concerned about her.

It was about an hour's drive to Encino. I took Sunset Boulevard to Hollywood and crossed Cahuenga Pass to the valley. As I raced along Ventura Boulevard, Scottie asked about "Daddy." I told her that he was well and working hard on a novel that he really believed in. I described the house. She would be able to use the pool at the Horton Manor. She might have to take driving lessons, I warned. She thought that was a good idea— better than going half way across the city to take tap dancing which he had insisted on during her last visit. She had never understood his reason for that as she had neither talent for nor interest in tap dancing, even though she adored Fred Astaire.

We arrived. She looked around approvingly. I called out to Scott as we entered and he came down the stairs.

"So you found her," he said.

They both seemed a little on guard as they hugged and I took my leave quickly. It was Saturday. They would have the weekend to face up to each other.

By Monday, the mood was easy. Scottie was around but not in the way. I don't recall anything unusual. Scott was more restrained in his behavior—polite and impersonal. My hours were more regular. When I asked Scottie about that summer, her memories were vague, too, but her feelings were positive. As she put it, "When he wasn't drinking he was awfully pleasant." And it was the best time she had had in California.

She showed him a short story she had written. He was proud and very helpful with criticism. The next summer the story was published in a magazine called *College Bazaar*. He was pleased and wrote his critique. "You've put in some excellent new touches and its only fault is in the jerkiness that goes with a story that has often been revised." He continued with some advice: "Stories are best written in either one jump or three, according to length. The three-jump stories should be done on three successive days, then a day or so for revise [sic] and off she goes . . . . However, I'm glad you published this one. It was nice to see your name." It shook him up, though, to see the feminization of his name in print and he said, "You calling yourself Frances Scott Fitzgerald [as if he hadn't named her] does push me into the background . . . and is likely to lead to a certain confusion. What do you think?"

At other times during the summer, Scottie said, he spent hours reading Keats and Shelley out loud to her. She sat through the sessions but was more bored than inspired, and was greatly relieved when a couple of Baltimore boys came through and phoned. Scott took them all to a nightclub.

Another visitor was a cousin from St. Paul, David McQuillan who entertained them at the Ambassador Hotel's palm-tree-decorated Coconut Grove that featured Big Bands and dinner dancing.

But mostly, they sat around and talked a lot. There were no major flareups. Scott did insist that she change

roommates for the next year. Scottie offered no contest.
She was, despite his apprehension, a clear-headed young
woman, not given to stubborn argument. She was
devoted to him and concerned about his health. She had
even agreed not to smoke until her nineteenth
birthday—an arbitrary year—and somehow kept happily
afloat in his sea of dos and don'ts.

She signed up for driving lessons. In between
sessions, I would take her out in the Ford to practice.
Or, if she had to go into town, I would let her drive part
of the way. We talked about living in Los Angeles—how
different it was from the East. It would have been
cheaper for her to go to UCLA but it would never have
occurred to Scott to send her there. She had to go to a
good eastern school. Also having her live underfoot
might have proven too much for both of them and
California was really just a stopping-off point.

Before she left, she passed her driving test. Scott
would no longer have to worry about her ability to get
behind a wheel and drive herself home in an emergency.
It had been a better visit than either of them anticipated
and they enjoyed each other.

When she returned to school, the tone of his letters
changed—somewhat. He threw himself into her Vassar
activities as if they were his own Princeton days. When
she wrote him about her participation in a musical
comedy group called OMGIM (Oh! My God, It's
Monday), loosely organized along the lines of the
Princeton Triangle Club, he answered, "You're doing
exactly what I did at Princeton. I wore myself out on a
musical comedy for which I wrote book and lyrics." He
then proceeded to sing his doom and gloom warnings:

how he slipped back in his studies and lost a year in college. She was to keep her scholastic head above water: "to see a mistake repeated twice in two generations would be just too much to bear." But when her play was heralded, he was able to say, "Now that it is over, I can admit that I thought it was quite a conception from the beginning and quite an achievement—I just had a moment when I was afraid that you were wearing yourself out over it."

So Scott reverted to custodian—but on a more acceptable level—warning, yes, pointing out the worst, then proud and loving, asking to be forgiven for doubting her. He seemed to carry within him a secret pain. When she came through unscathed, he was relieved and told her how glad he was. And indeed he did have the deep and agonizing fear of Zelda's illness and his own alcoholism at the root of all his uneasiness about Scottie. He tried to erect a barrier that would make her immune to neurotic contagion, that would make her the one right thing in his life. And he was overbearing in the process. He redefined boundaries at each new stage of her development—behavior, manners, education, men to date, men to marry. He set standards to serve her according to his formula for her growth and happiness.

She did not come back to California in the summer of 1940. She went to Harvard Summer School instead. Scott was impressed by her bent toward "study." But Scottie said it was more of a lark than a serious educational effort. If anything, it was a good way to meet Harvard boys. Scott reminded her that John Reed came out of Harvard. It was his way of alerting her to the caliber of Harvard men.

■   ■   ■

Early in 1940, Scott suffered his first mild heart seizure.
While trying to open a window, he raised his arms and
felt a sharp stab of pain that took his breath away. It was
followed by a stiffness in the arms. He phoned the
doctor who came out promptly. It was not a heart attack,
but Dr. Nelson said it was a warning that he might have
an attack if he did not take care of himself. Scott so
understated the incident when he confided it to me, that
I didn't take him seriously. He didn't dwell on his weak
heart or use it the way he did his T.B. flareups. But he
did worry about a recurrence. He had enough leftover
religion lurking in the recesses of his soul to feel that he
was being punished for abusing his body; and he was
determined to get back into grace in his own ways—
ways that would conserve his energy and give him the
time necessary to finish his work. He decided to give up
living out in the country and to move closer into town
to eliminate the strain of driving. He took an apartment
on Laurel Avenue in West Hollywood, just a block away
from Sheilah Graham's place, which eliminated the
long trek from the valley. It was a "garden court" group
of flats which meant that you walked past a little patch
of grass to get to the front door. Scott's place was set
back from the street and was on the upper floor of this
two-story L-shaped building. It was light and airy, had
an adequate living room furnished in tasteless period
English. There was also a dining-room, a small kitchen
and a bedroom. Scott did nothing to enhance the decor
other than to set some books out. He didn't seem to
mind the impersonal environment. All he needed was a
place to work and enough room to pace. It had that. I
set up in the dining room.

The apartment building was fairly quiet except for periodical bursts of laughter and screaming—sometimes maniacal, other times joyous. After a few such outbursts, Scott made some inquiries to the manager. It turned out that there was a woman tenant who laughed and screamed professionally for radio, and practiced regularly. Once the reason for the commotion was revealed, Scott was no longer bothered by it. At least she was neither insane nor wildly happy. Scott was not a laugher. I don't think I ever heard him laugh out loud. He seemed rather to smile deeply.

Though he now looked more frail than usual, he didn't run a temperature nor was he wracked by coughs, though he would make mention of both in his letters. The heart condition intensified hypochondria. He was a chronic taker of temperature. Any coughing he did resulted from cigarettes which he smoked incessantly. He took a B complex vitamin regularly. He was worn out and doubly anxious about all his unfinished business. He drove himself to keep going, but it took a great deal of energy that he was unable to spare. He was such an insomniac that he had to spend a good deal of time in bed during the day. His meals were light. I would fix bacon and eggs for breakfast if he woke late and was hungry enough, and the usual canned turtle soup for lunch. Dinner was the larger meal. Nothing fancy—steak or chicken, usually prepared by a part-time maid whom he shared with Sheilah. They ate together every night—either at his place or hers.

The drinking was under control. He hadn't stopped completely. Scott, of course, did not fix himself a drink, so it was hard to tell. I never saw the bottle until it was discarded. And from the small number of bottles that were trashed since the move, his consumption appeared to be minimal.

■   ■   ■

We had just about settled in when Scott got an offer to do a screenplay. Once again, the novel went to the back burner. However, this was a project that Scott was enthusiastic about. It was the adaptation of his short story *Babylon Revisited.* The deal was negotiated by agent William Dozier who was with the Berg-Allenberg Agency. The independent producer who wanted to do the film was Lester Cowan. There was no big Hollywood money offered—only about $5,000 with more to follow upon completion of the screenplay. But on the asset side, Cowan respected Scott and was sensitive to *Babylon*'s poignant quality. Also Scott would be working on his own material from start to finish rather than adapting another writer's idea. He would not have to buck big studio interference nor sacrifice his attachment to the characters.

The plot dealt with Charles Wales, an alcoholic who, after the death of his wife, lost custody of his little daughter to his sister-in-law who accused him of responsibility for the tragedy. Wales went on the wagon in an effort to regain his child. He was unsuccessful.

It was a story Scott knew from deep inside him, one that parallelled his life. True, Zelda hadn't died, but a part of her had. Scott never lost custody of Scottie, but he was an easy mark for family critics and the fear of being the only one responsible for raising her was easily transferable to the fear of losing her.

The story rekindled old fires, but he was far enough away in time to be able to handle the material objectively while retaining its original dramatic power.

Lester Cowan was a slight, dark-complected man with the look of a bantamweight boxer: bashed-in nose, tough. Outwardly they were an unlikely pair, yet Cowan was a Fitzgerald fan and they had good rapport; at least they were in agreement on the direction the screenplay would take. Cowan would come over to the apartment every few days to thrash out the development of the scenario. They would talk for a couple of hours. I would fix them a simple lunch—soup and a ham and cheese sandwich on toast—while they conferred. Then Cowan would leave and we would get to work.

The screenplay was an area of writing for which Scott abandoned his customary pencils. He preferred to dictate. Scott was the writer, the actor, the director. And it was a one-man show. He paced back and forth—more of a shuffle in his backless slippers. Despite the mild climate, his outfit was a sweater or robe over shirt and slacks. As he paced, he talked, gave directions, grew animated, intense, sad, nervous. He expanded the taut story to a highly-charged play in which the hero was the victim of his embittered sister-in-law's wrath. She was angry, accusing—if he hadn't neglected his wife, she would not have died—she was determined he would never get a chance to neglect his daughter.

The love between Charles and little Honoria, the reunion and ultimate separation were theatrically fool-proof and though there were unabashed teary elements; there was also a strong, sympathetic portrait of the alcoholic father which carefully kept the balance on the side of poignancy rather than melodrama. Cowan wanted Shirley Temple for the role of the child. Scott had met her and thought her an unspoiled, bright little girl, though a bit old for the part.

■   ■   ■

Scott's invalidism disappeared when he was doing what he liked to do. His energies soared and his creative mechanisms needed little rewinding. Periodically, he would go into the kitchen, get himself a coke, and bottle in hand, go back on the treadmill. He must have worn a path in the carpet. The pacing was the only exercise he took and it was probably good for him.

Sometimes he would rest in the afternoon, which gave me a chance to type up what he had dictated. Other times, if the work had gone smoothly, he was too exhilarated to rest and would wander through the apartment or come lean over my shoulder to see how a scene read. His hovering made me nervous and I would suggest that he find something to do. With exaggerated apology, he would move over to the window, smoke a cigarette, stare into space and talk about women of beauty. Zelda had been the most distinctively beautiful in her early days; movie starlet Lois Moran, the inspiration for Rosemary in *Tender*, was a fresh beauty. Loretta Young with her delicate "teacup" face and Norma Shearer's classic profile were added to the list. He was incurably romantic, forever reaching for an elusive fragment of love, forever conjuring up illusions. He would ramble on about the dramatization of his work. He thought *Babylon* was a natural for film. *Gatsby*, on the other hand, hadn't made the transition to film successfully (1926) and he commented with some irony that the one play he had written, *The Vegetable*, didn't make it from an Atlantic City tryout to the New York stage.

I only half listened to him because, though he was talking to me, he was also waiting for the script. As soon as a segment was finished he would go over it and if he liked it would phone Cowan and read it to him. He would wave me over to the phone to watch his performance. Scott, looking like a matinee idol who had seen better days, would give such a touching portrayal that Cowan would dissolve in tears at the other end of the line and Scott would cry at his end. After he hung up the phone, he would turn to me in a diabolical change of mood and tell me how good it felt to have wrung some tears out of a producer who was underpaying him. I was an appreciative audience for his act.

His mood was proof that the project was good for him even though the screenplay, renamed *Cosmopolitan*, was not produced during his lifetime. Cowan had difficulty getting sufficient backing and eventually sold it to MGM. It was "rewritten" for Elizabeth Taylor and Van Johnson and outrageously violated the original script.

■   ■   ■

It was late fall in 1940 before Scott was able to give full attention to *Tycoon*. This time he would stay with it to the end. The essentials that had been churning inside him for so long were written in his head. The characters were defined and Scott could walk them through the chapters to see how well they followed the story line. He had not definitely decided how he was going to resolve the romance between Kathleen and Stahr and there were other loose ends. Scott knew he would be reworking the book many times before he would be satisfied with it. But it was now urgent that he get it all down on paper.

We established a routine. He turned out pages every day and I typed—first in triple-spaced drafts giving him ample room for making corrections, then retyping in double-space and then, likely as not, another retyping for the possible "first" draft.

We managed to keep this semblance of order going and Scott began to feel good about the progress he was making. On occasion, he took time out to worry about the war in Europe and to rechart army tactics. When he wasn't playing general, he was coaching football. He would make lists of team players and put them through the plays that should have made them winners. I didn't know enough about football to discern how successful he was, but I do know that he kept losing the war in Europe.

His penchant for organized game playing was just another extension of his list making. It amazed me that he could expend so much energy on war maneuvers and sports. But he found it relaxing, a reason to put odd pieces together, to solve problems and even come up with a winner now and then.

■   ■   ■

At one point during these months, Sheilah went out of town to attend a film opening. Scott disliked eating alone and asked if I would come to dinner with my younger brother, Morton, who had tried his hand at a short story that Scott had read and commented on some months earlier.

We met at Victor's Restaurant on Sunset Boulevard, a short walk up from Scott's place. Scott played the gracious host and ordered a bottle of wine. He went into great detail about French chateaux and their products, identifying the vintage from the bad years. This was all new to Morton, who was a minor and not a drinker. This also left a full bottle to be consumed, which made me uneasy. There was no way I could have suggested that we skip the wine. Scott would have taken that as a personal affront, an implication that he couldn't control his alcohol. Certainly, I wouldn't say anthing that might embarrass him in front of my brother.

Throughout dinner, Scott did most of the talking. He sipped the wine and chatted about Hemingway who, he said, owed a debt of gratitude to Ezra Pound and Gertrude Stein for their criticism of his early work, which influenced his style. The wine began to take effect and Scott relaxed enough to vent his irritation with Ernest. He called him a poseur who was trying to prove his manliness by going off to Spain and Africa in pursuit of adventure. He was running dry and had to search out experience just to have something to write about.

Scott began to ramble. He got sentimental about Princeton and its influence on him. He said it was a blend of the best of both sides of the Mason-Dixon line—northern learning and southern chivalry.

By the end of dinner—and the bottle of wine which Scott finished—he was glowing. He asked us back to his apartment. Once inside, he boldly brought out a bottle of gin in a gesture of hospitality. This was the first and only time I had ever seen him display the bottle. We both refused drinks; he filled a glass for himself. He talked about Morton's interest in writing and encouraged him to keep at it, to dig deeply for the "intimate self" that would help him find his style. He was convivial with glass in hand, even as his eyes grew glazed. I became concerned about the effect the gin was having and suggested that we leave. I used Morton's morning class at Los Angeles City College as an excuse. Scott, always polite, thanked us for coming and walked us to the door.

Morton was really impressed and charmed. Scott had treated him like a young *writer* and had talked to *him* about Hemingway. He would never forget it. I was somewhat less enchanted and was worried that the visit would set off another binge. Would he keep drinking for the rest of the night? I didn't want to think about such a possibility.

The next day, I went to work prepared for the worst. Amazingly, Scott was up when I arrived, and there was not a trace of the previous evening's indulgence. He had gone to bed after we left and slept it off.

I was relieved particularly because Sheilah was due back and if she had found visible signs of regression she would have been horrified. She needed to feel that she was responsible for his sobriety. And in a sense, she was. They had worked out a relationship that was peaceful enough to give him the mind to work and to make escape to full time alcholism unnecessary. She diligently

continued reading the books from the lists that Scott
prepared for her. They discussed the books, had dinner
at home, at the Brown Derby in Beverly Hills or at
Victor's. They listened to records. My older brother,
Nathan, is a musician and Scott asked him to suggest a
series of classical recordings to supplement the
literature. Scott wanted Sheilah to have an appreciation
for all the arts in their appropriate time frame. Theirs
was now a stable pattern—no longer of news value for
the local trade papers.

■　　■　　■

As the writing progressed, letters to and from Scottie
were friendly. She suggested that he read Thomas
Wolfe's *You Can't Go Home Again*. He was not as
swept along by it as she was. He thought the Great Vital
Heart of America was corny but did admit that the book
"doesn't commit the cardinal sin: it doesn't fail to live."

He wrote to her about men—the kind to marry—
men in journalism or law who lead rather larger lives—
a man "who is not too much a part of the crowd."
When he listened to the broadcast of the Harvard-
Princeton game, he wondered if she was there. There
was a nicely expressed warmth between them. She
wished he could come east and meet her boyfriend,
Samuel Lanahan, a Princeton senior. She was sure her
father would like him. Scott was never able to make the
trip, but Lanahan was the man Scottie later married.

Scott was on a respite from money worries as long
as he continued to live economically. He had no
problem about cutting back expenses. His beautiful and
damned spendthrift days were over. He no longer had a

desire to attract attention to himself except through his writing. He did want to secure his reputation with his peers and his readers and he hoped the new book would do this for him. Yet despite the mood of calm, I have a dark impression that lingers—of a walk we took up the street at one day's end. I was going to my car; he was going on to Schwab's Drug Store on Sunset Boulevard, just a couple of blocks away. He was wearing a dark topcoat and a grey homburg hat. As we kept pace, I looked over at him and was chilled by his image, like a shadowy figure in an old photograph. His outfit and pallor were alien to the style and warmth of Southern California—as if he were not at home here, had just stopped off and was dressed to leave on the next train.

■　　■　　■

In contrast there were the active, productive highs that made everything seem right. A memo with a precisely itemized list of instructions and trivial household needs was so reassuring to me.

> Dear France:
> Here is the order of the work in case Papa is too exhausted to think.
> Before I start dictating this morning:
> a) Everything I dictated under financial transaction as far as you can get.
> b) What the lawyer said.
> c) Characters
> d) Outline Scenes 1-149
> After I finish dictating what I have dictated (149-end) takes precedence over c) and d).

On the back of the page he wrote:

Ask me about:
Will you tell laundry to pick up. Also trousers and repair.
Ask me about Mildred and keys
About grocery check.
Your check.
Did you ask about vitamin B.
Need coin purse, cheap tray,
Drop Books
Need cigarettes and large bottle Lavoris
Need pencils

Scott

The first part of the memo referred to scenes he had outlined for the novel and a chapter reorganization. The remaining items were chores. Mildred was a cleaning woman who came twice a week. Pencils had to be knife-sharpened by hand (by me) so he could bear down on a blunt point without snapping it. There was always a little list.

Favorable winds prevailed and Scott sailed along through the fall season. The day after election, November 5, 1940, I was awakened by a telegram:

SLEEPING LATE STOP STUFF ON DINING ROOM TABLE HOORAY FOR ROOSEVELT AFFECTION SCOTT.

We stayed on course toward a solid first draft of *Tycoon.* He had made almost half a dozen starts, and after each interruption he rethought and reworried and

Dear France:.

Here is the order of the work in case Papa is too exhausted to think.

Before I start dictating this morning:

(a) Everything I dictated under financial transaction as far as you can get

(b) what the lawyer said.

(c) Characters

(d) Outline Scenes 1 – 149

after I finish dictating what I have dictated (149–end) takes precedence over (c) + (d).

(over)

(2) ask me about;
Will you tell laundry to pick up. Also trousers + repair.
ask me about Mildred + keys
about grocery check.
your check.
Did you ask about vitamin B.
Need coin purse, cheap tray, ..
Drop Books
need cigarettes + large bottle Savoru
need pencils

rewrote. He kept putting Cecilia (the narrator and daughter of the producer who was Stahr's enemy) in and out of a sanitarium. Perhaps if she were ill, he thought, her narration would be more sympathetic. He made little pencil notations in the margin: "re" was a short reminder to himself to rewrite.

He experimented with titles: The first working title was *Stahr: A Romance*; then he toyed with *The Love of the Last Tycoon: A Western*; *The Last of the Tycoons* finally became *The Last Tycoon*. Which would he have stayed with? Scott was a great changer. It is possible he would have given it still another title. His aim was to make it his best work. This had to be the definitive novel on Hollywood.

It would be nothing like *What Makes Sammy Run?*, which had been recently published. Its author was Budd

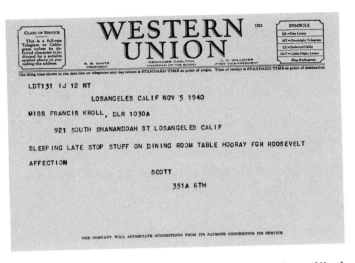

Schulberg, a young Hollywood writer whom Scott liked personally, even though they had had a disastrous collaboration on a screenplay for a film called *Winter Carnival*. Scott was relieved, after reading Schulberg's book, that it would in no way threaten his own *Tycoon*. Budd's was a rather blatant portrait of one kind of filmmaker, he thought. His own focus would appraise the antagonism between the creative and corporate interests and bring a grander scale to the Hollywood story. Nonetheless, he acknowledged *Sammy* politely.

■   ■   ■

Just when Scott was working at his best, he began to have warnings—rercurrent spells of dizziness. I never witnessed them, but he would describe to me how he would stand up and suddenly have to grab for some support. The condition became serious enough for the doctor to prescribe bed rest, and Scott moved in with Sheilah. She had a ground floor apartment with no stairs to climb. She also had a spare bedroom. It made sense that he should accept her offer and not be alone at this time. It was a temporary arrangement as Sheilah also used her apartment for an office, and had a full-time secretary. The household was busier than Scott was accustomed to.

Scott obeyed the doctor's orders to a point. He refused to interrupt the pattern of his work and continued to turn out pages daily. I would pick up the draft at Sheilah's, then go over to his apartment to do the typing and take care of any necessary chores. I would return the copy to him at the end of the day so that he could rework it in the evening.

Scott asked me to look for another place to live in the same neighborhood. In early December, 1940, I found a charming walk-in bungalow on Fountain Avenue, nicely furnished, that would be available after the first of the year. He signed the lease. I picked up cartons from the local market and started packing books and papers in preparation for the move.

In the midst of the confusion of these changed living patterns, Scott suddenly became aware that Christmas was coming. He had no idea what he could do for Scottie. Sheilah volunteered a fur coat that she had hardly worn. It needed restyling and shortening, and they both wondered if my father would consider remaking it into a more youthful design. Pop came up with a charming style and remodelled the coat without charge. Sheilah and Scott were delighted. I mailed the fur off to Scottie. Scott promptly wrote her a letter suggesting that she write thank you notes to Sheilah, my father and me. Then he pencilled a note to Pop for me to hand deliver.

Saturday, December 14th

Dear Mr. Kroll

    I want to add my thanks to Scottie's for the beautiful cutting of the coat. It is perfectly magnificent and we are so happy to have it. Not having seen her for fourteen months I took pleasure in imagining her face when she got it— her surprise and delight.

    It was a grand Christmas present, much greater than I would have been able this year to give her myself . . . . .

    With all good holiday wishes

Sincerely
Scott Fitzgerald

P.S. The pencil is the result of writing in bed for the present.

■   ■   ■

The Saturday before Christmas—December 21, 1940— was cool and overcast, on the gloomy side. I stopped by Sheilah's in the morning to bring Scott the mail and some typed manuscript pages. There were two letters for him to sign—one to Scottie, another to Zelda. He was sitting up in bed and was in good spirits even though he said he hadn't slept well. He asked if I had checked the bureau drawer where he had some cash tucked away in a book in case anything should happen. The money was still there, I told him. Besides, what could happen? He shrugged. He was less tense than he had been at any time since I came to work for him and I even commented on how "rested" he looked. He smiled in an odd, skeptical way. Was there anything else he wanted me to do for him? There was nothing. Just post the letters and enjoy the weekend. "See you Monday," I said, as I went off to do some holiday shopping.

When I returned home, later that afteroon, there was a message for me to go to Sheilah's immediately. I was not to phone, just to come. Seemed strange. I dashed out of the house and drove to Hollywood wondering what could possibly be so important at 4:30 on a Saturday afternoon. The door to the apartment was open. I rushed in and just as quickly drew back in horror. Scott was sprawled on the floor. Two attendants stood near him with a stretcher. Sheilah was sobbing and being comforted by a woman I didn't know. Scott just lay there, fully dressed in tan slacks and plaid jacket. I was utterly bewildered. Had he fainted? Was he unconscious? I moved in closer—and I knew. How did it happen? I pleaded.

Sheilah quieted momentarily and told me that she and Scott were sitting and talking after lunch when he stood up, grabbed the mantle and then just keeled over. She tried to revive him, but he was gone. I couldn't absorb it. "He was fine when I left him" was all I could say. There were no further answers. As the men prepared to remove the body, the woman (who turned out to be Buff Cobb, Sheilah's friend and granddaughter of Irvin Cobb, a popular humorist) took Sheilah out of the room.

I just stood there disconsolate. The apartment was

suddenly bleak and cheerless. I felt out of place and helpless. I wandered into the dining area to ask Sheilah whether there was anything I could do. She shook her head. Buff would look after her. Sheilah told me that she had already phoned Harold Ober, who would tell Scottie. Someone, probably Judge Biggs of Delaware, would get in touch with me. She looked at me and said, in her English accent, "Poor Fr*ahn*ces."

I left in a daze and drove home, trembling in aftershock. It's amazing I didn't have an accident. I was unable to get the final inert image of Scott out of my head. I was unprepared for the reality of *dead*, especially as he had underplayed the seriousness of his heart condition. I was so accustomed to underestimating Scott's ailments and categorizing them all as hypochondria, or as a coverup for drinking, that I was angry at myself. But maybe he hadn't dared acknowledge the legitimacy of his condition even to himself. This was one time he did not cry "wolf." Why didn't he? Was he frightened? Was there anything we could have done to prolong his life? I had not experienced such a loss before. Although my grandparents had died when I was a child, they were old and it was expected. But to say goodbye to Scott so casually in the morning and be summoned to the silence of his death was like being jolted out of a bad dream and discovering it wasn't a dream. What would happen now? What would happen to the novel?

■　　■　　■

The ensuing hours would have been unbearable were I not immediately plunged into taking care of the necessary details of closing out his life.

Judge John Biggs of Delaware, Scott's Princeton classmate and executor, phoned me that very evening to ask if I would make the mortuary arrangements and have the body sent to Baltimore for burial. Would I also collect and store Scott's possessions, vacate the apartment and send him an accounting of monies and property on hand? He would phone again and would put me in touch with a Los Angeles attorney. There was no one else familiar with Scott's affairs, and there was no question that I would do whatever was required. The only light note for me was remembering Scott's elaborate test of my honesty when he first hired me. I was the only one who knew that he had hidden $700 in cash.

Squeamish about facing up to the mortuary visit alone, I asked my brother Nathan to come with me. I gathered up some burial clothes. Scott had recently bought a Brooks Brothers suit—his first piece of new clothing in over a year—and its dark color seemed appropriate for the occasion. On Sunday, the day after Fitzgerald died, we drove down to the Pierce Brothers Mortuary on West Washington Boulevard in an old, downtown district of Los Angeles. We entered the hushed environment and were greeted by one of the servants of the dead. I explained that we had come to make arrangements for F. Scott Fitzgerald and turned over the clothing. We were then ushered into the coffin mart. Rows of boxes sat on display in a variety of finishes with a range of interior linings from pink satin to purple plush. I wondered what he would be happiest in for that everlasting duration. I was sure my predicament would have amused him, and I could hear him laughingly suggest purple for his purple prose or white for his pure soul. The choice was finally determined by the amount of money I had to spend. Something simple, grey with a white interior. The cost was $440 plus transportation. The bill came to $613.28—just a little short of the $700 he had set aside. Had he phoned to find out what the cost would be so he could leave the right amount? I shuddered at the thought.

The following Wednesday, after they had "laid him out," I went back to see him. It was a disturbing, melancholy visit. The figure in the grey box had no connection with the Scott I knew. The mortician's cosmetics defaced him and he looked like a badly painted portrait, waxed, spiritless, with unlikely pink cheeks. How still he was. Like a mannequin in a store window. Why wasn't he shuffling about, moving papers around, lighting a cigarette, pacing restlessly? This deep quiet was out of character. Was he asleep at last? Without a phenobarb? I was certain that he was not at peace. How could he be, dying before his work was done?

I sat in the cell-like room alone with the body in the open coffin trying to keep some continuity going. "What will you do, when the book is finished?" he had asked me one day. He was concerned that he might not be able to afford me, that he might have to return to the East. I was touched by his thoughtfulness and told him not to worry, that I could find another job if he would give me a written reference. He had kidded me that he couldn't promise what he would say; and I said he would just have to fake it. Well, he had pulled a fast one. He was going east ahead of schedule and he'd not even given me notice.

I stared at him for a good while wondering what had been in his mind in those final moments. He must have had a premonition that he was fighting time. Otherwise why would he have kept that cash at home instead of depositing it? But had he really been ready? Had he been seriously thinking about death since the heart attack? Or was he so taken by surprise that there were no last thoughts?

I was overcome with feelings of grief and frustration. He had been on the downhill slope of his career and now everything was over. The book that he believed would bring him back to the attention of the reading public was a profusion of manuscript pages and notes. All that anxiety and wasted energy, I thought. And he, dressed in his best suit at what should have been his peak years, was going away—never to return. I took a lingering look and tried to memorize a face that was no longer his. I whispered "Goodbye" and left him to make his journey.

■   ■   ■

The next day, I let myself into his apartment. It was eerie. I sat in the living room in one of the chairs upholstered in a mottled fabric ("vomit green" was Scott's description of the color). Everything was so dreary and sterile—just another flat without Scott to enliven it. I shuddered, then forced myself to go into his room to start sorting his belongings. Difficult as it was, it served as a healing ritual and it took several days of going back and forth. I made an inventory of everything and filled his trunks with books, clothes, notebooks. I scanned the miscellaneous jottings that would ultimately find their way into print and become perennial quotes. I labeled the trunks and cartons and listed the contents.

I half expected him to walk through the door and ask for the list to make sure I was packing everything properly. Then a stream of disconnected memories brought him closer. There was the time when I asked whether he would like to have his car washed. He joked back, "Oh, you haven't the time to do such chores, Frances." I thought of the middle-of-the-night phone calls when he couldn't sleep and wanted to talk. To avoid disturbing my family, I would pull the phone into the bathroom, sit on the edge of the tub and listen until he got tired. Sometimes he would tell me that he had sent me a telegram to be delivered the next morning, but in case it didn't arrive on time would I stop to pick up the laundry first. Another time, he asked if I knew anyone who was still reading him. Why was he writing this book if there wasn't anyone left who would read it? I assured him that college students knew his work well. He was part of American literature studies. How did I know? Because my brother was a student and he told me. Scott, temporarily placated, would apologize for phoning so late. Goodnight. Goodnight.

■   ■   ■

There was no time for mourning. On December 22, 1940, Sunday, after the trip to the mortuary, there were two phone calls from John Biggs with a list of instructions. He also gave me the name of a local lawyer (Barry Brannen) to consult and to whom I could turn over any necessary documents. The following correspondence ensued:

Sunday, December 22, 1940

Dear Judge Biggs:

In accordance with our telephone conversation of today, I am enclosing a copy of Scott's Last Will and Testament. The penciled changes which you will note on pages 1 and 7 of the Will were made by him on November 10, 1940. Whether they were legally witnessed I do not know, but I see no additional witness names so I do not believe that anyone was present when these changes were made. However, I copied the Will as it was originally and made the changes exactly as he did on the original in ink.

Also I am enclosing a statement of the bills which are due and owing. This is not a final statement but will give you an idea of the state of his affairs. There will undoubtedly be other small household bills like grocery, laundry, pharmacy, etc. And probably an additional bill from his doctor, Clarence Nelson. The Scribner Book Store bill that I have is through July and when I find the later ones I will add them on, and send a complete, corrected statement to you.

I have in cash $706.00 of which I am using $613.28 for burial expenses—

Casket and service	$410.00
Shipping	30.00
City Tax	1.50
Transportation	171.78
	613.28

I will hold the balance of $92.72 until I hear

further from you. The body will arrive at 6:56 a.m. on Friday, December 27, and will be sent to William J. Tichnor & Sons-Mortuary, North & Pennsylvania Avenues in Baltimore.

I will go to the insurance company tomorrow (Sun Life Assurance Co.). I've tried to locate the policy but cannot find it. I will go through the entire file carefully again tomorrow. I can't imagine what happened to it unless Scott put it in some hiding place. However, I will wire you about it. I do have his insurance folder with some receipts and the policy number (#112346) but the information concerning the status of the policy is also missing. I made every effort to contact Barry Brannen today but it was not possible. However, I shall get him the first thing tomorrow morning so that he can advise me the best possible way to act, in order to avoid snares and also have him look into the insurance matter as well as the executor matter . . . .

I will keep in close touch with you and await word from you concerning the personal possessions of which I will send you an itemized list tomorrow. Please feel that you can count on me for anything and I will try to be of as much help as possible at this end.

> Most sincerely and with deepest sympathy for the loss of your good friend.

P.S. I held this letter until this morning and have this additional information concerning the insurance. It seems the insurance company is holding the policy against a loan, but so far as I was able to gather the policy is in good standing and the amount payable is $44,184. I am on my way down to see Mr. Brannen now and will write you further this afternoon.

I also recall two personal debts which are not in writing but which I am sure Scott would have liked to take care of and they are to Gerald Murphy, New York City in the amount of $150, and Maxwell Perkins in the approximate amount of $1,000.

Of Scott's outstanding debts, the largest was to Highland Hospital for Zelda. He had made periodic payments, but he had never been able to clear the balance. Other small items like $7.12 (one of Scottie's purchases) to a New York department store and $10 to a skin doctor reveal how stintingly he budgeted petty amounts of money in order to manage living expenses. Juxtaposed against the fortune his writing has since earned and continues to earn for his heirs, the impoverished estate he left behind makes its own ironic commentary.

I enclosed the following list of accounts payable with the letter to Judge Biggs:

BILLS TO BE PAID

Scottie's Bills:—

B. Altman & Co.		
Balance owing from March, 1940	$34.33	
Franklin Simon's		
Balance owing from Sept., 1940	7.12	
Dr. Hamman		
Balance from July, 1939	25.00	
Edythe Harris Lucas		
Balance for dress from July, 1940	20.00	
Dr. Norburn		
Operation in June, 1939	200.00)	
interest on above	14.00)	
Dr. Wolff		
Balance for skin treatment		
from August, 1939	10.00	
	310.45	310.45

Zelda's Bills:—

Drs. Sinclair & Barker		
Balance for dental care from 1939	28.00	
Jean West		
Balance from 1939 for dress	26.12	
	54.12	54.12
Highland Hospital	4117.14	4117.14

Household and Personal:—

Bay Cities Laundry		
(Encino Balance)	33.10	
Hollywood Bookstore	47.74	
Dr. Howson		
Balance from 1939 (one visit)	65.00	
Master Pest Control—balance	9.00	
Monumental Storage (Baltimore)	202.42	
Dr. Clarence Nelson	25.00	
	382.26	382.26

Scribner Book Store (?)	153.77	153.77

Miscellaneous:

Authors League—March, 1940	$ 52.50	
Community Chest—1939	125.00	
Class Fund—Oct. 1939	10.00	
Screen Writers' Guild—Balance	57.50	
University Cottage Club	20.00	
	265.00	265.00

Income Tax:—

1938—State of Calif. (Balance)	301.69	
1938—U.S. Government (Balance)	585.23	
	886.92	886.92
Total		$6169.66

Additional Bills:

Dr. Charles J. Welker	4.00	
Dr. Norman F. Crane	5.00	
Pierce Bros.	440.00	
	$449.00	
Arden Farms, Inc.	.69	
Hollywood Laundry	3.91	
Ley Bros.	15.98	
Southern Calif. Edison Co.	1.10	
Subtotal	21.68	
Schwab's Pharmacy	16.08	
Crescent Hts. Market	13.90	
Subtotal	51.66	
So. Calif. Gas Co.	2.97	
Total	$ 54.63	

Regarding the Pierce Bros. Mortuary balance—Judge Biggs asked that I just pay the transportation charges until further instructions.

IN ACCOUNT WITH

MISS FRANCES KROLL
921 SOUTH SHENANDOAH STREET
LOS ANGELES, CALIFORNIA

Pierce Brothers
720 West Washington Boulevard
Los Angeles, California

FUNERAL EXPENSES OF   F. SCOTT FITZGERALD

DECEMBER 23, 1940

TO CASKET AS SELECTED, TRAVELING CASE AND
PROFESSIONAL SERVICES   440.00

CASH DISBURSEMENTS:

CITY TAX   1.50
TRANSPORTATION CHARGES   171.78
     613.28
CREDIT BY CASH   173.28
     440.00

On December 26, John Biggs sent me a wire:

> WILL RECEIVED STOP PLEASE GATHER TOGETHER
> ALL BANK ACCOUNTS CHECKBOOK CANCELLED
> CHECKS AND SIMILAR PAPERS AND HOLD UNTIL
> FURTHER INSTRUCTION THANK YOU.
> JOHN BIGGS JR.

And on December 31, I wrote him that I had
everything intact:

> Dear Judge Biggs:
>   It seems that the bank is returning all checks,
> even if they were issued a week or more before
> Scott's death, as a result of which the bank balance
> is $738.17. Among the checks that were issued and
> will be returned were rent, $85., the last payment of
> 1939 income tax amounting to $137.63 to the U.S.
> Government and $66.74 to the State of California.
> Also there will be closing utility bills like
> telephone, light and heat. I have not yet received
> those statements. . . . There is a small grocery bill

of $13.90 and one that was paid by check which will be returned of $11.64. If you would like me to pay these by cash please advise . . . .

I have stored everything in the Hollywood Transfer and Storage Company at the rate of $2.75 per month. The cost of moving was $6.00 plus $2.75 for labor connected with storing. I have, however, not yet paid for this and am not touching any of the cash on hand until I hear from you. The only payment was salary to the maid for $14. and my salary for one week which Miss Graham said she spoke to you about and which she insisted on my accepting.

Scott's possessions in storage consist of:
1 trunkful of clothes
4 crates of books
1 carton of scrapbooks and photographs
1 small trunk with some personal effects, like the last Christmas presents sent him, personal jewelry, other trinkets, several scrapbooks and photographs
2 wooden work tables, lamp, radio
There is also a 1937 Ford which I am keeping in my garage at home. The book value of this car is about $300.

I received a wire and letter from Mrs. Fitzgerald asking me to send her Scott's personal effects. Shall I do so? . . . . Awaiting your reply, I am

Most Sincerely,
Frances Kroll

Biggs' answer was brief:

All of Scott's things will have to be kept intact and
not even his personal effects can be given to Zelda
until the executors have qualified and they give
you permission. We will probably know within the
next few days whether we will qualify in
California or in Maryland. I will communicate
with you just as soon as the decision is made.

■   ■   ■

The formality of the law was upheld, but letters and a
phone call from Zelda followed like plaintive cries. She
had been so removed from Scott in actual being—living
in her strange, imaginative, confused world. Her illness
caused her to leave him much before he was ready to
give her up. And so she remained to him—alive but
inaccessible—a constant shadow.

Yet, Zelda knew he was there for her, and she counted
on him to say yes or no, to argue with, to defy, to accept,
if only by mail. Now there would not even be the letters.

On Christmas Eve, I was at home when the phone
rang. It was Zelda calling from Montgomery where she
was staying with her family while on a temporary leave
from Highland Hospital. She said she needed to talk to
someone who had been with him at the end so that she
could *believe* he was gone. (She did not know about
Sheilah or at least could not acknowledge that there
might have been someone else in California.) She
grieved, she said, that he had been so far away and alone
at the end. Her voice was calm, liquid with the hint of a

southern accent. I assured her that Scott had died peacefully and was working until the last; that I would take care of all the details. She was effusive in her thanks.

I felt a great sadness for her, sorry for her terrible unfinished feeling of never having said goodbye. Maybe there is no way to say it, but those who live on wish they had been able to offer the rite of comfort. And for Zelda, particularly, her last parting from Scott after the disastrous Cuban holiday had been such a chaotic scene.

A poignant letter from Zelda followed our phone talk.

> Dear Miss Kroll:
>
> Again, I express my gratitude to you for all your kindness to my husband. Though I knew that he was ill, his death was a complete shock to me, and so heart-breaking that I am inadequate to his last necessity for me.
>
> My husband did so much for other people. Many nights I have known him to sit up over another manuscript when his own was not completed; and one of my most happy memories are the times he spent lost in interest and enthusiasm for the work of a prospective author. He was as generous spiritually as he was materially and I am sure that he left many friends behind.
>
> If you would be kind enough to communicate whatever details of his death are at your disposition, and to write me an account of the service in California you assuage a heart laden with pity and regret and gratitude and do a most charitable act.

My husband's lawyer: Mr. John Biggs, Jr., Wilmington, Delaware, will assume financial responsibilty and see that your accounts are straight. I know that Scott would have wanted you to have some little testimonial of your kindness so when I have access to any money, I want to send you something. This will be later, of course.

I am grateful to God that I still have my daughter. Life is almost endurably sad without the inalienable ties that soften its inescapable tragedies.

That's why I feel even worse that my husband should have died out there alone and am so reiterant about the appreciation of your sympathy and efforts.

    With kindest regards
             Zelda Fitzgerald
             322 Sayre St.
             Montgomery <u>Ala.</u>

The concern for me in the midst of her sorrow moved me to tears. I sat awhile and reflected on the intense and tragic quality of their love. Rent apart as their marriage was, the essence of what they once meant to each other had not been lost to her until now, and the letter contained a measure of emotion that no illness could touch. Though Scott's obligation to Zelda always came first, he had not died alone. He had found some consolation in a new love. It was she who was alone now.

As for the hope of some tribute to Scott out here, there never was one. He was not really a part of Hollywood.

Dear Miss Kroll:

Again, I express my gratitude to you for your kindness to my husband. Though I knew that he was ill, his death was a complete shock to me, and so heart-breaking that I am inadequate to his last necessity, for me.

My husband did so much for other people. Many nights I have known him to sit up over a thesis manuscript when his own was not completed; and one of my most happy memories are the lunches he spent, lost in

interest and enthusiasm for the
work of a prospective author.
He was as generous spiritually
as he was intellectually and I
am sure that he left many
friends behind.

If you would be kind enough
to communicate whatever details
of his death are at your dis-
position, and to write me an
account of the service in
California you assuage a
heart laden with pity and
regret and gratitude and
do a most charitable act.

My husbands lawyer:
Mr. John Biggs, Jr.
Wilmington Delaware
will assume financial
responsibility and see that
your accounts are straight
I know that Scott would have
wanted you to have some little
testimonial of your kindness
so when I have access to any
money I want to send you
something This will be later,
of course.
I am grateful to God that
I still have my daughter. Life

'ts almost unendurably sad
without the inalienable ties
that soften its inescapable
tragedies.

That's why I feel even
worse that my husband
should have died out there
alone— and am so
reiterant about the ap-
preciation of your sympathy
and efforts

With kinder regards

Zelda F. Fitzerald

322 Sayre St.
Montgomery Ala.

One more letter from Zelda followed:

Thank you again for your kindness. Time passes and I still half believe that I will be hearing on Monday from California. Life descends like the dropping of a portcullis instead of the promise of a garden gate when good friends die and one is bereft of the happy haven of a heart that cared.

Memories are more poignant than they are irrecapturable.

Since Mr. Biggs is in communication with you, of course his procedure is authorative.

There were little things, notebooks, the old worn Thesaurus that I would like to have.

Meantime, again I thank you—and express my kind regards and good wishes.

Zelda Fitzgerald

Jan. 13

The next several weeks were spent scurrying about winding up odds and ends. There were statements to fill out for insurance; there was a problem with Scott's apartment. The company that owned the building wanted to bind the estate for rent until they found a new tenant. I turned to Mr. Brannen, the attorney, for help. Finally, I relinquished all papers to him. My work was finished—reluctantly.

Then, in January, Scottie sent a note:

Dear Frances: January 21, 1941

I am writing to ask if you would do me a great favor and I hope it is not too late. There were some

322 Sayre St
Montgomery
Ala

Dear Miss Kroll:
Thank you again for your
kindness. Time passes and I
still half believe that I will be
hearing on Monday from California. Life descends like the
dropping of a port cullis
instead of the promised a garden
gate when good friends die
and one is bereft of the happy
haven of a heart that cared.
   Memories are more poignant
that they are irretrievable.
   Since Mr. Biggs is in
communication with you, of
course his procedure is authorative.
   There were little things.
note-books, the old worn treasuries
that I would like to have.

   Meantime, again I
thank you — and express
my kindest regards and
good wishes
         Zelda Fitzgerald
Jan. 13.

people, the Turnbulls, in Baltimore who lived next door to us and who were very devoted to Daddy. Mrs. Turnbull wants very much to have something of his, like a penknife or a paper weight or something like that—maybe even just a pencil. If you still have not disposed of everything I would appreciate it so much if you would send her a little something . . . . Thanks so much for doing this. I appreciate it so much—please mail it collect.

Love,
Scottie

The note was so appealing, I wished I could send whatever she requested. Instead, I had to write her that everything had gone to storage and that after Judge Biggs made his legal determination she would be able to find a souvenir among the stored possessions. I was struck by the trail of warmth Scott left behind so that a memento—even a pencil—would have such sentimental value for a friend.

How Scottie learned of Scott's death is a scene that might have been written by him if he had plotted the drama of his last exit.

On that Saturday night, December 21, before Christmas, Scottie was at a party given by a Vassar classmate. She was dancing when Dick Ober, son of Harold Ober, cut in on her. They had always had a sort of grudging brother-sister relationship and Scottie said to him jokingly, "Something vital must have happened for you to be coming to a party to see me."

"It did," he said. Then he blurted out, "Your father died tonight of a heart attack."

Scottie thought it was a bad joke. She could not believe what she heard. "Daddy?" she asked. Impossible. If that was some kind of teasing, it wasn't funny. He solemnly assured her it was true. There was no easy way to break such news and he handled it the only way he could—directly. He took her home to the Obers.

The irony of getting the tragic news at a party escaped her at the time. Their relationship was sadly unfinished and she had no awareness then of how much she would miss him. Certainly she felt shock, but she was not allowed to feel either forlorn or abandoned. Scott's extraordinarily loyal friends—the Obers, the Perkinses, the Turnbulls—immediately formed a protective circle around her, a solid embrace that held fast until she was ready to walk alone.

Like most children, she had assumed he would be there forever or at least long enough to see how she turned out. The echoes of Scott's hopes must have played a part in the woman she became. She married the "breed" of man Scott suggested. Her first husband was a lawyer, her second was in politics. She raised a large family—four children. If not by actual design, she found that parental anxieties were more equitably distributed in a larger family. In the process of dealing with her own brood, she began to understand Scott's demands of her as an "only" child.

In all, the values he deluged her with had a lingering effect. Concerning her own brief time with "Daddy," she regrets that she was not more aware of his talent. She "vaguely perceived him as some kind of genius who had fallen on hard times." And indeed he was and had. But if they had had more time together, more time to talk; if she had asked more quetions about his writing and paid more attention to what he was saying, would it have been enough?

The ifs have passed us by: if I had kept a workday diary; if Scott had known he wasn't going to finish the novel; if he had finished it, would he have been heralded or would his critics have been carping? All are unanswerable. There are not enough years in a lifetime for parents and children to understand each other or for artists and critics to accommodate each other's views. But for Scottie there are the letters and the estate of F. Scott Fitzgerald—an estate that worked its way up from poverty to riches as this very fallen genius was rediscovered by succeeding generations of readers—a heritage that reaches out to his grandchildren and great grandchildren.

How Scott would have appreciated that success— that measure of immortality he strove for. I can see him bowing politely to accept the award of recognition. Literary, financial and family absolution.

AFTERWARDS

IT MIGHT have been over. The chores were done. There were still the phone calls from reporters asking questions. Some of the young ones thought Scott Fitzgerald had long since been dead. They weren't really interested in the last quiet years and I had no interest in giving them sensational copy. There were a few writers who knew better.

The *Los Angeles Times* ran a short, sensitive piece on the editorial page in December, 1940:

> Almost as if he were typifying his uncertain and groping generation even in his early death, F. Scott Fitzgerald has passed from a world gripped again by the same kind of war hysteria that first made him famous . . . .
>
> Fitzgerald had an importance—only time will tell whether it was ephemeral—because he made himself the voice of youth crying in the wilderness of political and social and moral muddling . . . .
>
> He was a brilliant, sometimes profound, writer. That his work seemed to lack a definite objective was not his fault, but the fault of the world in which he found himself. He was left a legacy of pertinent questions which he did not pretend to be able to answer. That was not the smallest part of his greatness.

And in the *New Republic* in the same month:

> Nobody else wrote about the American aristocracy of the post-war years as did Scott Fitzgerald. Nobody else could make it seem glamorous while retaining his integrity as a literary craftsman and his clear-sightedness as an observer. The heroes of his early novels and short stories were boys who had gone to the right prep schools and made the right eating clubs at Princeton. The heroines were girls who had won their freedom in the excitement of wartime, who had learned to smoke and neck and take nips out of pocket flasks, with a general air of glitter and defiance . . . .
>
> All that seems a very long time ago . . . . His death there [Hollywood] for anyone who was young in the 1920s, is like the death of one's own youth. It is like a stone placed over the grave of all the flappers and smoothies, all the glitter and foolishness and wild good humor.

It wasn't that I preoccupied myself with obituaries but I was at loose ends and I kept looking for acknowledgements of his place in 20th Century literature. There was still no assurance that *The Last Tycoon* would ever see print. After Scott died I had written a note of sympathy to Maxwell Perkins and though his answer was encouraging, it was too soon for him to indicate any publication plans. He had not read a word of the manuscript until Sheilah Graham sent

him the copy that was in her apartment early in
January. But before that time, Perkins wrote to me:

Dear Miss Kroll: December 31, 1940
    Thank you ever so much for your letter about
Scott. I know how you will miss him, like all of us
who knew him well. The most tragic thing about
it all is that the book was not finished. Sheilah
Graham told me a great deal about the state of the
manuscript yesterday. Perhaps there are parts of it
that could be published separately in some fashion,
in periodicals. But it would have been at least the
equal of any book Scott ever wrote, and a kind of
vindication before a public that thinks of him now
as one who wrote frivolously. The truth is he had
an amazing talent, as everyone knows who has read
all that he has written. But he did get to be
associated with the age which he named. It was
because he succeeded so well and that then his
work was for so long interrupted. Anyhow, I am
glad he did not have to go through a long illness,
and suffering.
    There seems to be considerable confusion
regarding the will, of various kinds, but I'll not say
anything about that for John Biggs has it chiefly
in charge, and I know he is in touch with you.
    Perhaps something will bring you to New York.
If it does, please give me the pleasure of seeing
you.
                            Ever sincerely yours,
                            Maxwell E. Perkins

■   ■   ■

By the end of January, John Biggs, who was scheduled
to come West to qualify as executor, was unable to make
the trip. He arranged things so that he could handle the
details in the East. At the same time, two of my friends
were planning to drive to New York and asked me to
come along. The idea was suddenly appealing. I did not
know what I wanted to do in Los Angeles. I was not
ready to attempt to work for another writer and though
I was attached to my family, it seemed the right time to
go back to New York. I also had a duplicate of the
manuscript which I had kept, pending word from Biggs
on estate matters, and though I certainly could have
mailed it, my friends agreed to stop in Wilmington so I
could meet the Judge and deliver the unfinished *Tycoon*
to him.

We reached Wilmington the second week in
February of 1941. Biggs was a big, somber man, a
prototype of a judge. He had been shocked by Scott's
death and wanted to know again how it had happened.
He was proud to have been named executor and would
see that Scottie and Zelda were taken care of. I gave him
Scott's battered old briefcase with the manuscript and
other papers. He was very moved—as if this were all that
was left of his old friend. We said goodbye in sadness.

In New York, I found a place to live on West Eighth
Street in Greenwich Village, and was quickly caught up
in the vitality of the city. I was home again. I renewed
old acquaintances, and then mustered up the courage to
telephone Maxwell Perkins. He was instantly available
and asked me to visit him at Scribner's on Fifth Avenue.

When I got to the store, I asked a clerk where I could find Mr. Perkins and was directed to his office.

I was transfixed as he extended his hand and looked me over. His eyes twinkled and his long, lean face was ruddy. His manner reminded me very much of an older Scott. The room fit my notion of what an editor's office should be—walled in by books, a desk piled with manuscripts, a warm shelter from the outside world.

We talked of Scott and those final months and how much he wanted to see *The Last Tycoon* in print. Perkins said he was still thinking through how best to bring out the incomplete work. He would let me know as soon as he decided. He was sure it would be published in one form or another.

He then became paternal and expressed concern about my being alone in the city. He wanted to know if I intended to remain and if I had any job prospects. If not, he would call John Marquand who was beginning a new novel and might need some assistance. He would make inquiries. At that point I wasn't sure how long I'd be able to stay on. Nonetheless, he said he would call Marquand. His thoughtfulness so buoyed me up that after I left the office, I started down Fifth Avenue and before I knew it, I had walked the whole distance home—from mid-Manhattan to the Village—almost three miles.

The job didn't pan out; Marquand had just hired someone. But I did pick up some temporary work, quite unexpectedly. I went to a beauty shop for a haircut and sat next to a genteel, middle-aged woman who was waiting her turn. We struck up a conversation and she mentioned that her son-in-law worked for *Time*

magazine. She suggested that I call him to see if they
had an opening. I felt that would be an imposition, but
she insisted. "We all have to help each other," she said.
The son-in-law was John Hersey, an associate editor. He
was polite, asked me to come in to talk and I learned
that he had been a secretary to Sinclair Lewis. We had
an amiable chat. There was no opening at *Time*, but he
sent me over to United China Relief, an organization set
up to help Chiang Kai-Shek, and a pet project of Henry
Luce. They hired me as a secretary-at-large. It was an
adequate stopgap. I was not committed to any one
individual, but I was in an office with bright, amusing,
young people all on loan from *Time*. I thanked Hersey
for the recommendation, but never saw him again.

■   ■   ■

Then in late April, Max Perkins dropped me a note:

> We are to publish the unfinished novel as edited
> by Edmund Wilson together with "The Great
> Gatsby" and a selection of the best of Scott's
> stories. I think it will be an impressive book as
> presented with an introduction by Wilson, and I'll
> see that you get a copy as soon as it is
> manufactured, which will be early in the Fall.
>
> With all good wishes, I am,
> Ever sincerely yours,
> Maxwell E. Perkins.

I was gladdened by the news that *The Last Tycoon*
would finally be in print. Once again Perkins had come
through for Scott.

CHARLES SCRIBNER'S SONS
PUBLISHERS
597 FIFTH AVENUE, NEW YORK

April 28 , 1941

Dear Miss Kroll:

Thank you ever so much for
your letter of the 24th. I am very
glad indeed to know that you have found
a position, and I hope it is a properly
remunerative one. We are to publish
the unfinished novel as edited by Edmund
Wilson, together with "The Great Gatsby"
and a selection of the best of Scott's
stories. I think it will be an impressive book as presented with an intro-
duction by Wilson, and I'll see that
you get a copy as soon as it is manu-
factured, which will be early in the
Fall.

With all good wishes, I am,
Ever sincerely yours,

Maxwell E. Perkins

Just about this time, Sheilah Graham came to town and invited me to lunch with Scottie and Edmund Wilson. The name "Bunny" no longer suited Wilson. He was rotund and had a forbidding personality. I, at least, was in awe of him. He told us that he was going through Scott's notes and would select pertinent ones to be published along with the original chapters. He would also summarize the end of the book, drawing on Fitzgerald's outline.

Both Sheilah and I talked about what we thought Scott tentatively intended, and he listened with a slight air of superiority. But for Sheilah, Scottie and me it was a pleasant reunion. There was the common bond of Scott whom we all missed in our own way and it was warming to share a moment together.

Then in May, Wilson wrote:

> Dear Miss Kroll: I am having Scribners' send you a copy of my synopsis of the unfinished part of Scott Fitzgerald's novel. Would you check it and let me know whether you can add anything or have any criticism?
>
> Yours sincerely,
> Edmund Wilson

I could hardly wait. When it arrived my reaction was more emotional than objective. I didn't know what to expect, but I had hoped for a more dramatic finish. Instead, it was a concise summary and, for me, not one to stimulate excitement in the novel. I was in a quandary. Wilson, after all, had an impressive reputation and a weighty presence in the literary world,

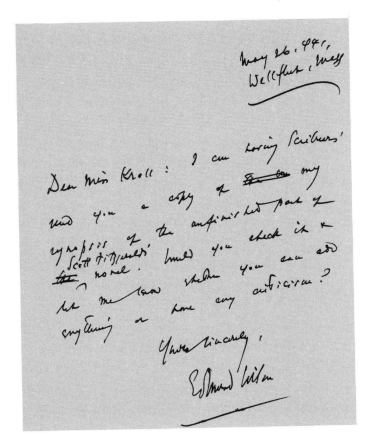

May 26. 1941,
Wellfleet , Mass

Dear Miss Kroll : I am having Scribners'
send you a copy of ~~the~~ my
synopsis of the unfinished part of
~~the~~ Scott Fitzgerald' novel. Would you check it &
let me know whether you can add
anything or have any criticism?

Yours sincerely ,

Edmund Wilson

but I felt I had to be honest, so I dared offer suggestions.
Certainly all those months of Scott's planning were still
fresh in my mind.

I wrote to Wilson:

> I've read and reread your synopsis. I think you've developed a wonderfully clear plot line, considering the mass of notes you had to wade through . . . . I feel that after reading the book, to plunge into several pages of outline will not carry through to the end any emotional contact with Stahr. Of course, I realize that the purpose of the synopsis is to give the reader an idea of the way the novel might have continued, but I strongly felt the need of a little padding of Stahr even in a synopsis.
>
> The story of Hollywood is not as important as is the conception of Stahr, the man.
>
> Although Scott definitely told me he did not want to make Stahr a hero in the conventional sense of the word and did not want to justify Stahr's manner of thinking, he did want to present it thoroughly and show the cause of Stahr's reactions. Stahr truly believed that because he quickly climbed the ladder from office boy to executive that all other people had the same chance for success . . . Despite Stahr's genius and artistry he did not "come along" politically.
>
> He believed in infinite loyalty—if you gave people a chance they should play along with you no matter what opposition they might have to your tactics. That was why he quarrelled with Wylie White [writer] whom he had repeatedly given a chance despite White's pranks and drunken habits and who turned [against Stahr] after the pay cut even though Stahr had not instigated this cut. I

think, too, it should be emphasized how badly
Stahr felt about the pay cut. Brady took advantage
of Stahr's absence from the studio to call a meeting
of the writers. With a tearful speech he told them
that he and other executives would take a cut if the
writers consented to take one. If they did, it would
not be necessary to reduce the salaries of the
stenographers and other low salaried employees.
The writers agreed to take the cut and Brady about-
faced and slashed the stenographers salary to a new
low anyhow. These are tactics which Stahr's sense
of fair play would never have allowed.

You mention something about Stahr's change in
status as a producer. Unless this is specified in the
notes, I don't think this is so. From what I
remember . . . Stahr was to make one artistic
flop—the kind of picture that would not be a
movie "box office hit" but one that would be an
artistic achievement. It was to be a picture in good
taste and perhaps filled with all the ideas Stahr, the
artist, has always wanted to see realized on the
screen, but which Stahr, the Hollywood producer
could not very well make because such a film
would not be money-making. It was to be a picture
he knew from the start would "lose a couple of
million" but which he nevertheless makes to
satisfy himself despite opposition from other
studio financial heads . . . .

Forgive me for running on like this, but I truly
think a few colorful background facts will make
Stahr more memorable even though so much of the
novel has to peter out in synopsis form.

If my suggestion has no merit, please just forget it, and if you think it might help, I know your expert critical hand will simmer this letter down to a few sentences rightly inserted . . . .

Wilson was good enough to answer (June 16, 1941):

Dear Miss Kroll: Thank you very much for your letter. I'll use some of your suggestions which help fill out the figure of Stahr. I have somewhat supplemented the text by including as much as possible of Scott's notes . . . . I'll have Scribner's send you a copy of the book which is supposed to come out in the fall.

> Yours Sincerely,
> Edmund Wilson

When the book was published, Perkins sent me a copy. I opened it nervously, sat down and read through it. I was both stirred and traumatized. The conclusion remained spare and, for me, a terrible letdown after the sweep of language that preceded it. If only Scott had been able to finish the writing even in a rough draft.

My personal disappointment was relieved, partially, by the inclusion of many of Scott's original notes. At least they reflected some of the emotion that went into the planning. Fitzgerald had left himself instructions to "Rewrite from mood. Has become stilted with rewriting. Don't look at previous draft." And he aspired "to give an all-fireworks illumination of the intense passion in Stahr's soul, his love of life, his love for the great thing that he's built out here . . . He's not interested in it

June 16, 941,
Wellfleet.
Mass

Dear Miss Kroll: Thank you very much for your letter. I'll use some of your suggestions, which help fill out the figure of Stche. I have somewhere supplemented the text by including as much as possible of Scott's notes about the character. — I'll have Scribners send you a copy of the book, which is supposed to come out in the fall.

Yours sincerely,

Edmund Wilson

because he owns it. He's interested in it as an artist because he has made it." Scott hoped the novel would be "something new, arouse new emotions . . . it is an escape into a lavish, romantic past that perhaps will not come again in our time."

My reservations aside, the critics seized upon the work as if it were indeed the last novel by the last of the novelists. The *New York Times Book Review* gave it front page coverage. Said reviewer J. Donald Adams, "It is a heavy loss to American literature that Scott Fitzgerald died in his forties . . . . Even in this truncated form *The Last Tycoon* not only makes absorbing reading, it is the best piece of creative writing that we have about one phase of American life—Hollywood and the movies."

Stephen Vincent Benet wrote in the *Saturday Review of Literature*: "As it is *The Last Tycoon* is a great deal more than a fragment. It shows the full powers of its author, at their height and at their best . . . . This is not a legend, this is a reputation—and, seen in perspective it may well be one of the most secure reputations of our time."

James Thurber wrote in the *New Republic*: "No book published here in a long time has created more discussion and argument among writers and lovers of writing than 'The Last Tycoon.' Had it been completed, would it have been Fitzgerald's best book?"

In *The New Yorker*: "Wilson's foreword is brief and unsatisfactory. One hopes he will sometime do a monograph on this man who hardly deserves to be ticketed as the laureate of the Jazz Age and then forgotten . . . . [A] careful reading of even this truncated

section of 'The Last Tycoon' persuades me that
Fitzgerald was on the point of becoming a major
American novelist."

■   ■   ■

So—Scott was back in print. The book was not a best
seller, but it was being read and reviewed by discerning
followers. His peers acknowledged his grace and his
place among them. That might have been enough for
him but there was more to come—much more.

Eight years passed. The interest in Fitzgerald that
was set in motion by Scribner's publication of the
unfinished *Tycoon* spiralled beyond expectation. A rash
of articles analyzing and defining Fitzgerald's place in
American literature appeared in "little" and literary
magazines—*The Arizona Review, The University of
Kansas Review, The Saturday Review*. His works that
had been out of print eased back on store shelves and he
became a major source of material for the insatiable
appetite of that new medium—television. Short stories
were adapted for half-hour shows and lost their quality
in the process. One critic described them as murky. I
recall an early television adaptation of *Gatsby* with
Robert Montgomery which failed miserably. But it was
the start of Scott's lucrative life after death.

It was not until 1949 that a full-length, serious
biography was written—*The Far Side of Paradise* by
Arthur Mizener. I first learned of Mizener's plan to write
the book when he tracked me down and asked for
information "in connection with Fitzgerald's daily life
and habits of work in California." I answered his
questions as best I could and promptly received a

request for more. I'm not sure I replied. By this time, I was involved in a new life in Los Angeles. I was married, had a baby and it was bothersome to get back into detailing bits and pieces of the past. We had no further correspondence. The Mizener biography stimulated further interest in Fitzgerald, who became a popular doctoral subject. Hardly a year passed without a student or scholar writing or phoning to research Fitzgerald in Hollywood.

Of all who came or called, Andrew Turnbull seemed most genuinely intent on writing a biography that would be true to the Scott he had known. From the time the Fitzgeralds left his parents' estate, La Paix, he had maintained a correspondence and friendship with Scott and Scottie. In April, 1961, when his *Scott Fitzgerald* was completed, he sent a note: "My whole book is pro-Fitzgerald. I wrote it because he seems to me a finer man than most people realize."

Following Turnbull came another bandwagon of writers singing their own speculative Scott Fitzgerald song, many of them off key. The boom continued up to the 1970s when Matthew J. Bruccoli, a professor at the University of South Carolina, came on the scene and took control of the Fitzorama. We exchanged some twenty-odd letters checking out details of *The Last Tycoon*. Though all this documentation has kept the Fitzgerald name in the stream, the mystique continues inexplicable to all but those whose lives Scott touched.

■   ■   ■

For me, that job of chance was a turning point. I have come a distance since then—marriage, two children, work at one form or another of writing and editing. Yet, through the years, Scott Fitzgerald has not been far behind. He has appeared with his never-written letters of reference each time I have been considered for a job and his complicated, sensitive, heroic person has had a dominant influence on my course. I have tried to keep the association in perspective in seeking my own identity, but I have carried from him a respect for the labor of writing as well as for the anguish of the creative process. Remembrance of the courage with which he moved himself out of his suffering into a final burst of activity that secured his literary image is woven into the web of my days, even as that time of my life recedes.

AUTHOR'S NOTE

THE SOURCE for this memoir is, of course, my own experience. I have however, referred to other works on Scott Fitzgerald's life and letters when a direct quote seemed to illustrate best my remarks. While my intention was not to enter into a scholarly dialogue, the published material about Fitzgerald has served to sharpen and confirm my view.

I am thankful to the Princeton Library for letting me browse through papers and absorb an environment that meant so much to Fitzgerald.

I am especially grateful to Scottie Fitzgerald Smith and Scott Berg for their encouragement and gracious contributions. There are also others to thank: Jack Langguth, Jon Bradshaw and Norman Jacobson for asking questions that needed answers; Bob Samsell for sharing his Hollywood conversations; my brothers, Nathan and Morton Kroll, for being there then and now.

F.R.

NOTES

21 "By rule of hour." From *Art* by Alfred Noyes.

28 "frighteningly gentle, with consummate grace." Unpublished interview by R.L. Samsell.

28 "never at home." Unpublished interview by R.L. Samsell.

32 "You were a peach." F. Scott Fitzgerald, *Letters*, ed. by Andrew Turnbull (New York: Charles Scribner's Sons, 1963) p. 105.

37 "I wish I was in print." Fitzgerald, *Letters*, p. 288.

42 "No hard feelings." Matthew J. Bruccoli, *"The Last of the Novelists": F. Scott Fitzgerald and the Last Tycoon* (Carbondale: Southern Illinois University Press, 1977) p. 36

44 "The afternoon was dark." F. Scott Fitzgerald, *The Pat Hobby Stories* (New York: Charles Scribner's Sons, 1962) p. 150.

54 "Dear Scott, we Mennonites." Matthew J. Bruccoli, Margaret M. Duggan and Susan Walker, eds., *Correspondence of F. Scott Fitzgerald* (New York: Random House, 1980) p. 533.

60 "He gave me some very helpful lines." Unpublished interview by R.L. Samsell.

66 "You can neither cut through." Andrew Turnbull, ed., *Scott Fitzgerald: Letters to his Daughter* (New York: Charles Scribner's Sons, 1965) p. 167.

67 "it's a fine novel." Fitzgerald, *Letters*, p. 311.

67 "What do you hear." Fitzgerald, *Letters*, p. 267.

79 "Do you want to come out." Turnbull, p. 91.

82 "interesting, surprisingly honest." Turnbull, p. 79.

83 "I send you a bonus." Turnbull, p. 119.

84 "at *Saturday Evening Post* rates." Turnbull, p. 57.

86 "You've put in some excellent new touches."
   Turnbull, p. 151.

87 "You're doing exactly what I did at Princeton."
   Turnbull, pp. 113-114.

98 "doesn't commit the cardinal sin." Turnbull, p. 158.

98 "who is not too much a part of the crowd."
   Turnbull, p. 158.

142 "Rewrite from mood." F. Scott Fitzgerald, *The Last Tycoon* (New York: Charles Scribner's Sons, 1941). Notes following the unfinished novel, p. 134.

142 "to give an all-fireworks illumination." Fitzgerald, *Tycoon*, p. 135.

144 "something new, arouse new emotions." Fitzgerald, *Tycoon*, p. 141.

English

The Novel

Bleak House
Tale of Two Cities   } Dickens
~~Great Expectations~~

Henry Esmond
The Virginians   } Thackeray
Vanity Fair
Pendennis

Alice in Wonderland
Alice Thru the Looking Glass } Carrol
Tess of the Durbervilles, Hardy
The White Company, Doyle
Tono Bungay, Wells
Youth's Encounter
Sinister Street   } Mckenzie
A Portrait of the Artist, Joyce
Nocturne, Swinnerton
The Pretty Lady, Bennett
A Passage to India, Forster
The Moon and Sixpence, Maugham
The Sailor's Return, Garnett
    The Short Story

American

Roderick Hudson
The Europeans
Portrait of a Lady   } James
The Aspern Papers
Sister Carrie
The Financier   } Dreiser
The Titan
The Octopus, Norris
The Jungle, Sinclair
The Custom of the Country, Wharton
The Lost Lady, Cather
The Enormous Room, cummings
A Farewell to Arms   } Hemingway
The Sun Also Rises
The Maltese Falcon, Hammett
Sanctuary, Faulkner

The Short Story

Daisy Miller
The Reverberator   } James
Perfect Tribute, Andrews
Gardner Stones
The Cabala, Wilder
Three Lives, Stein

Youth
Heart of Darkness   } Conrad
Puck of Pooks Hill, Kipling
Dubliners, Joyce
Even Then, Baldwin
Lady into Fox, Garnett
The Woman Who Rode Away, Lawrence
Christmas Garland, Beerbohm

French
The Novel

Les Liasons Dangereux, Laclos
Le Rouge et Noir, Stendahl
Notre Dame de Paris, Hugo
Peau du Chagrin ⎫
Le Père Goriot ⎪
Eugénie Grandet ⎬ Balzac
La Cousine Bette ⎭
Mme Bovary, Flaubert
Thaïs ⎫
Le Lys Rouge ⎬ France
Aphrodite, Louys
À la Recherche du
    Temps Perdu (7 Books) Proust
Chéri, Colette
La Condition Humaine, Malraux

Short Story
La Sucette ⎫ Balzac
Trois Contes ⎪ Flaubert
Le Morceau de Ficelle ⎬ Maupassant
Le Rocher des Diables ⎪
La Maison Tellier ⎭

Other Literatures
The Novel

The Idiot ⎫
Crime and Punishment ⎬ Dostoevski
The Brothers Karamazoff ⎭
Anna Karenina ⎫ Tolstoi
War and Peace ⎬
Smoke ⎫
Fathers and Sons ⎬ Turgenieff
The Song of Songs, Suderman

Short Story
The Decameron, Boccaccio
The Cloak, Gogol
The Darling, Chekov
Death in Venice, Thomas Mann

Reading lists for Sheilah Graham

Drama + Poetry
Macbeth,
The Country wife, Wycherly
Importance of Being Earnest, Wilde
The Playboy of the Western world, Synge
Man + Superman
Heartbreak House   } Shaw
Androcles + the Lion }
Lyrics of Keats, Shelley, Marvel
        Byron + Dowson

Drama + Poetry
Pulitzer Plays
Lyrics of Poe, masters

Other
Wells Outline of History
Morton's Peoples History
Byron, the Last Journey, Nicolson

Other
Browne's Stranger than fiction
Life of Wilde, Harris
Flaubert, Mme Bovery } Sleepwalker
Ben Johnson
Art masterpieces, Craven
Van Loon's the arts
Ten Days that Shook the World, Reed
Lafargue's Property
Boon of Daniel Drew

Drama

Drama
The Doll's House } Ibsen
Hedda Gabler
The Cherry Orchard, Chekov
Plays of Molnar

General
{ Shelley by Maurois
  Proust's Life
  Renan's Jesus

General
The Apologia } Plato
The Phaedo
The Working Day et Mart
Song of Solomon
Ecclesiastes
Job   } The Bible
Matthew
Mark
Luke
Communist Manifesto, Marx + Engels
New Russia's Primer

Reading lists for Sheilah Graham

About the Author

Born in New York, Frances Kroll Ring moved to Los Angeles over forty years ago and grew up with the city. Her association with Fitzgerald led to work as a film story analyst, a book reviewer and a writer/editor of a California magazine. She is currently editing a quarterly at the USC School of Journalism. Each job prepared her for the one that followed, she says, but she had no preparation for raising two children and for being a grandmother, her most rewarding preoccupations.

FOL

DEC 2 9 2023